SAVING FRANCESCA MAIER

CLAIRE WINGFIELD

otp

ISBN: 978-0-9575279-4-2

www.offthepressbooks.com

For all the brief acquaintances who have touched my life – especially in the Berlin years.

1

They've had to abandon the taxi. Staggering with her suitcase in short, panic-fuelled spurts of energy, then gasping for breath – the morning air cold in her throat – Francesca knows her mother is silently blaming her. Her mother's words from the previous evening hang between them. 'Why on earth do you always need to bring so much with you? *Surely* you can't need all those shoes.' A silver trainer is now poking out of the top of her mother's hand luggage, its grubby toe pointing back at Francesca.

She hadn't meant to make them late. Her mother would never believe her in a million years, but Francesca is actually looking forward to this trip. It's a big thing her father is doing, taking her to his home country. She just hadn't known they

wouldn't be able to drive up to the airport this particular day. Lots of other people hadn't either apparently, and now Francesca and her mother are just
two more bodies in one anxious and strangely sad
trail, the path ahead littered with odd scraps of
clothing and abandoned belongings. There's a pair
of swimming trunks lying solemnly in the middle of
the empty road, every so often giving a tiny forlorn
flap in the breeze; a child's spotty raincoat snaked
around the bottom of a lamppost; a dismembered
sandwich waiting to be trod on. Francesca steps
carefully over the sandwich in her green open-toed
sandals and by now bedraggled summer dress.
Please don't let us miss this flight, she repeats like a
mantra. Their check-in slot is scheduled to close in
exactly twelve minutes, and Francesca still can't see
the airport building. It's hopeless, but she stumbles
doggedly on, following her mother who is striding
ahead, always just out of reach.

On any other day they would have reached the
airport ages ago, cleared check-in and security, and
had oodles of time to spare. Her mum would probably have bought her a treat – some jewellery or a
new perfume – from one of the duty-free stores.
They would be waiting to board already. So
Francesca absolutely can't slow them up any more
by confessing she is growing increasingly desperate
for the toilet. She wonders how long you can hold it

in before doing some kind of internal damage. She files the question as something to Google when this is all over. Carefully, of course – at fourteen, Francesca has learnt that there are some words you should never enter lightly into an internet search engine.

At least they don't have any children with them. The couple in front do, and a chubby little blonde boy in a pale blue surfer t-shirt is being dragged along screaming.

Up ahead, an old woman in a red and white tracksuit, her grey hair adorned with sparkling diamante slides like it's Christmas, has given up entirely. She sits on the wall outside a squat little house, her battered holdall relinquished on the ground below. Francesca wants to tell the old woman to take care of her things – you never know who's about – and to get up and come along with them. With a little effort, she might make it. Whatever she's given up on – a trip to see her grandchildren, an island-hopping Mediterranean cruise, home – might still be able to come true, if only the old woman believed it and started moving again. Francesca will help her. But as she draws level with the old woman, Francesca knows that to help would only slow them down and they'd have less chance of making it themselves. So she doesn't.

·   ·   ·

IMOGEN IS CURSING TWO THINGS. One: that Alex isn't here to help (though that's not unusual). Two: that she hadn't come into even fleeting contact with any of the many forms of media on which she might have heard the news this morning. This is unusual. She's normally right there on top of things. It's in her job description. She wishes Francesca would keep up. Really, at nearing forty you'd expect her to be the one lagging behind, not her teenage daughter. All anyone has said is that there has been an attack at another airport in the city. She hasn't asked for more – they have to get on. Running, staggering, walking, they have to get there. This isn't just a simple holiday for them – she daren't think what might happen if she isn't there to keep things under control. And if her knowledge of the morning's details is delayed, what does it matter? Once at the airport, she knows there will be no escaping the images of what has happened just a short time before. At least neither of them are nervous flyers. Imogen looks back at her daughter, refusing to countenance the idea that their flight might be cancelled.

'Come on, Fran. We're nearly there – I can see the terminal.'

'At least dad missed this. He'll be waiting for us with no idea what we're doing.'

Or he'll have heard the news, thinks Imogen. He

won't know which airport we're flying from, or even what time exactly we'll be flying. He's hopeless with details.

'He will be there – won't he?'

Imogen wonders about Francesca's doubt. Had she heard them arguing? Imogen can never be sure how much her daughter hears.

'Of course – it's us I'm worried about! Here, let me try something. I'm sure I can manage both suitcases.' With a suitcase in each hand, Francesca's school rucksack on her back, her own grey laptop bag in danger of strangling her, and swinging somewhere in between a little embroidered bag with both passports and all their valuables in it, Imogen pushes heroically on, brusquely overtaking the family in front.

Francesca follows close behind, offering up soft apologies in her mother's wake.

2

Anja is baking bread. She's polished all the mirrors, and taken out the recycling. She's placed an extra chair in the room for the girl. The flat seems small, cramped. It will seem smaller once everyone arrives. She's glad Richie and Alex aren't here to help but are off out somewhere picking up the easy closeness they'd enjoyed fifteen years ago. It was a blessing for all of them, really, that Alex had travelled ahead for his conference. She needs time to think. She likes time to plan a few conversations before guests arrive. For really, what do old friends talk about? Old friends such as themselves, who'd known each other for such a short, intense, period of time. She remembers Imogen is clever. Even with the language barrier. And this time, she supposes, with the girl here too, they will have to talk in English, and then she'll be at a definite disadvantage.

She decides to take down a picture in the living area, and then stares at the hole it's left, and the faint mark where it hung. She looks for something to put in its place, but nothing looks right, so she places a spray of silk flowers in the middle of the dining room as a new point of focus.

Imogen didn't want to stay with them. She could see it was Imogen's decision, when Alex had explained. The more natural thing would have been for them all to stay with her and Richie. They have a (small) spare room, and a sofa bed for them to pull out for the girl. It's that kind of break, a catch-up with friends, not a large-house-by-the-lakes family holiday. Still, if they have the money. And it's obviously the way Imogen wants things. She'd been almost shy when they'd met. Intelligent, but shy. Young for her years, too. She'd never have made demands, and had been sweetly delighted whenever her and Alex's plans had coincided when they'd first started dating. She'd never expected him to *want* to do anything for her.

Anja moves the flowers to the floor, then worries about Francesca knocking them over. Obviously she's not a child, but teenagers are clumsy. It's a reflex from the school, too. Her vocation of wiping things up, gluing things back together, of seeing ac-

cidents before they happen. She'll pull Richie across
the road sometimes, sensing volatility in a stranger's
walk. He always lags back, sulking at the tug of her
arm on his. 'Relax, sweetheart. Re-lax.' Richie is relaxed enough for the two of them, you can see it in
the way he poses in their sepia holiday shots. A
montage of summers spent in the Spanish country-
side, Richie's huge grin unchanging from year to
year – eager and unguarded, while Anja grimaces in
the too-bright sunshine.

She's ready for them now. She's even dressed in
her outdoor shoes and a scarf, although she's not
going anywhere herself. She sits, flicking through a
catalogue, signalling readiness, until she begins to
feel a little silly wearing the scarf – it's out of season,
and out of place. She couldn't look sillier if she were
wearing sunglasses inside. She gets to the children's
section of the catalogue, where there are five little
blonde girls who look like sisters modelling
wellington boots in the sunshine, and begins to
wonder if the others have met somewhere else
without telling her. Perhaps they've all decided to go
for pizza; perhaps Richie and Alex met with Imogen
and Francesca at the airport, and forgot to pick her
up on the way. Or they went to settle in to their
house at the lake, and Richie went along too, and
didn't think to call her. That would be typical of
him; of her lot. She's made potato and leek soup,

and rosemary bread. There's chocolate mousse for desert. Only a little something – it's an odd time for them to arrive. It's just like Richie to forget all about her. She knew he hadn't been listening when she'd discussed the menu choices with him.

3

'The girl opposite us was sick, dad. It was gross.'

'Couldn't have been very nice for her, either.'

'There was loads of it. And two stewardesses brought a trolley to try and clean it up, but they got it on its wheels and then it was trekked all the way up the plane when they went to take it back. I heard someone in first class was sick after that, too. *I* wasn't.'

'Glad to hear it, Fran. Well, you've met Anja. This is her partner, Richie.'

Francesca is suddenly embarrassed. She'd forgotten other people were there. Her father moves out of the doorway, and Richie reaches down and kisses her on both cheeks. It's not something she's used to, and she doesn't know whether to kiss him back, or where. He looks at her warmly. She grins back. She can feel his saliva on her cheek.

'Would you like me to heat you boys some soup? We already ate.' Anja is smiling, but Francesca can tell she's a little bit annoyed. She can sense that about people. Her mother is also ominously quiet. Francesca and her mother arrived by taxi an hour ago, having finally given up on her father arriving at the airport to collect them, or answering his voice-mail. It was terrible, waiting. Francesca knew her father would have a good reason for not being there to meet them, but still. Whenever Francesca started to say anything at all, her mother cut her off, telling her there was no need to worry – knowing Alex he'd probably just got caught up in something and was having a grand time.

Pretty soon, Francesca gave up and the silence between them stretched all the way back to the UK and the last row she'd heard her parents get into, late at night when they'd thought she was sleeping. Her mother had been punishing her father for in-sisting on making this trip, forcing them both to fol-low. At the airport, Francesca began to think that perhaps her father's no-show was just his way of punishing her mother back.

Without the two men, the flat felt like some-where waiting for a party to begin. It couldn't start without them, and Anja quickly retreated to the kitchen, leaving Francesca and her mother in the small, dark front room watching TV in German on an old-fashioned set, half the size of the flat-screen plasma Francesca has in her bedroom at home. They witnessed a very explicit ad for shower gel together. It was difficult to start talking again after that, so Francesca wandered over to look at a large fish-tank standing in the corner of the room. One of the fish seemed to be stuck to the side of the tank, its mottled grey-green skin flat against the glass. Francesca put her face up close to the fish's, squashing her nose against the cold surface of the glass.

'They're Richie's,' Anja said, walking through with a tumbler of lemonade for Francesca and a cup of English tea for her mother. 'He wanted a pet that wouldn't take much looking after, and my father suggested fish. That one's Emilio. Richie chose him right away – he thinks it's cool that Emilio sticks up against the tank like that. His lurker, he calls him. He loves that fish.'

'Emilio,' Francesca repeated, tapping lightly on the glass.

'Please don't do that, Richie says it can drive the fish crazy.'

Francesca stepped away quickly, tripping over

her apology, just as an everyday orange goldfish glided into view.

'I wonder what kind of behaviour a crazy fish would display? Seriously, I mean. We're looking at developing a new segment on animal behaviours at the moment...' Imogen leant forward, switched into work mode, one idea igniting another.

'I really don't know. Richie has some books,' said Anja, gesturing towards a small half-empty book-case before returning to the kitchen.

'That fish-tank is the only thing that has changed in here in fifteen years,' Imogen whispered slowly when Anja had gone, carrying a small stack of fish books over to the couch. 'Imagine that, Fran. It's all exactly like it was.'

Francesca likes the flat – they don't have any pets at home, nobody has any time to look after them – but concedes it's pretty small compared to their place. Her parents have moved four times since Imogen brought Alex back to the UK, each move into a bigger house in a better area, reflecting the sharp progression of their respective careers. Right now, her father is trying to buy another plot of land, so he can design their next residence himself. He's promised Fran a swimming pool.

Francesca knows her mother once worked with Anja – that she'd actually got her the job at the kindergarten, which Anja is still in, and her mother has long since left. It is all she really knows about her mother's time in Berlin. She'd never been able to think about it as a child. It made her giddy. A time before she was born. It was like trying to understand it was a different time of day on a different part of the planet. She'd learnt about the phenomenon, but she'd not wholly believed it until her first holiday abroad. And now, here were the people from that time – people who'd known her parents before they'd been her parents. People she'd only known as photographs, and had never thought to encounter like this – over chocolate mousse and rosemary bread, sudden kisses in a brand new city.

'So, princess, what would you like to do tomorrow? Which part of this crazy city would you like to see first?' says Richie, punctuating each sentence with a grin. *He means me*, Francesca thinks, her ears flushing.

'It is going to be hot tomorrow. Really hot. We should go to Wannsee,' Anja answers. She adds a sentence in her own language, twenty words which Francesca hears as one. Her father fires something back, and tomorrow's plans seem to be agreed. Francesca thinks how strange it is to see him so easily involved in another world.

Then her mother takes charge again, telling Francesca to get her things together before they set off for the lake house.

· · ·

IT IS early afternoon when Francesca wakes the next day, and she is disconcerted to see Anja in the kitchen with her mother. The room is washed an unfamiliar orange, light from the open window dancing on the border of terracotta tiles. Francesca had slept most of the way home last night, her first experience of the *S-bahn*, and fallen into the first empty bed she could find. She lingers in the arched doorway, adjusting to the brightness, tuning to the hushed conversation she is about to interrupt.

'It has turned out well for you, *na*?'

Her mother takes a second before answering. 'We are happy.'

'Then it was worth it.' For a moment, Francesca thinks she is still in bed, dreaming. *Worth what?* she wants to ask.

'Things haven't been so easy for me and Richie.' She gives a tiny, brittle laugh. 'You'll see it, I'm sure. Don't you ever wonder—'

'Francesca, you're up! I thought we'd never wake you. Hurry up and get ready, we want to go out.'

There's a sharpness to her mother's tone that strikes Francesca as deeply unfair. But more than that, Francesca hates to be hurried; her mum knows this. Years ago, they'd come to an agreement: Francesca was only to be hurried when she had to

be. If something could be missed. She doesn't believe the lakes are going anywhere, and blames this
strange woman for making her mother forget how
their family works. She walks slowly to the sink,
runs the cold tap and drinks from it. She can see a
silver sliver of lake through the window. Her mother
goes to the cupboard and hands her a glass.
Francesca places it on the worktop and continues
drinking from the tap. She's in her nightclothes in a
strange new place, and her parents have let people
in without telling her. It has always been just the
three of them, and Francesca has grown up valuing
her privacy, as well as her considerable influence on
the status quo.

FRANCESCA SULKS until they sight the beach. When
they do, she can't help but crack a great big grin.
There's a wooded sandy path leading down to what
Richie has told her is the biggest lakeside beach in
Europe. The sand is sparkling white and there are
pedalos and volley-ball nets; a slide mid-distance
out in the water; a chic café; and when she widens
her vision from the main stretch she can see that,
further along, the shore is spotted with shaded retreats where trees line the water's edge. Francesca
feels a pull in her stomach and begins to run to the
end of the path and across the already crowded

beach, kicking sand across a dozing man's enormous sunburnt belly. She doesn't notice him grunt and turn over.

The water is just the right kind of cold after the burning sand, and Francesca watches her parents and their friends set up camp on a good spot just above the crowds. There is a checked blanket her mother has brought from the house, and an improvised picnic basket taken from their landlord's bike. There is even a large orange canoe Francesca wasn't sure they should have taken. It had been tied to the roof of the shed, but Richie assured them all that it would be too much fun to leave behind, and her father had joined him in lowering it in its cat's cradle to the ground. Francesca had told them all that *she* wouldn't be using it.

There's a group of teenagers next to her family's settlement, and Francesca waits until they decide to come out to the water before leaving it herself. They take a long time to make a collective decision, one girl particularly unwilling to leave her belongings unwatched, but equally unhappy at the prospect of staying behind herself. *I'll watch it for you*, Francesca thinks. *Don't let yourself get left behind.* Finally, one of the boys grabs the girl's hand and drags her along the beach towards the lake. The girl pulls away laughing and races him to the water's edge. Francesca makes her move – not towards her family after all, but towards the quieter part of the beach, where a gentle lapping of water can be heard in place of beachside conversation. It's cooler here, in the shade, and Francesca breathes in the distinct smell of lake.

'You want to come out with me?'

Francesca turns, startled, and Richie puts his hand out to steady her. She is balancing on the roots of a tree, and he's carrying the orange canoe under one arm. Richie is wearing only a pair of flip-flops, some black swimming trunks and Ralph Lauren sunglasses – not at all like her father's haphazard beachwear. She tries not to look at Richie's chest. For some reason, it reminds Francesca of the top of her piano at home, and she has a sudden strange image of Anja polishing it.

'I'm not sure it was meant for us to take,' she says, sternly. She can't help but feel morally superior to a man who cares quite so much about his appearance.

'You are on holiday! This is for holiday.'

'It's like stealing.'

'Pah.'

Richie sets the canoe down in the water and climbs in. He looks up at Francesca. She looks down the beach towards the crowds, shrugs, and steps in to the canoe. She has rolled her jeans up to make shorts, and they get splashed when Richie begins to paddle – a great surge of power to get them away from the shore and out onto the lake. Richie is at once entirely consumed by the action of paddling and entirely at ease with it; a machine driving infinitely and unquestioningly forward.

They go beyond the swimmers, the slide, the pedalos, until Francesca thinks they are the furthest vessel from shore. The long holidays stretch in front of her luxuriously, and Francesca is happy. Richie is not out of breath when he stops paddling, and lets the canoe simply be afloat, a strip of darker blue separating them from the crowded broken waters ahead. He stretches contentedly and pulls his feet up onto the wooden ledge. He looks funny, and Francesca does the same. Richie grins.

'I always canoed as a boy. We'd race each other, and I always won.'

Francesca smiles in the gap he has left her.

'You don't speak German? I'm surprised.'

'I used to be afraid of it.' She doesn't know this is true until she says it. 'I used to say to myself that dad had been body-snatched, and that's why he was talking this weird language I couldn't understand. When I was small I used to cry and scream when I heard him speaking it on the phone. I'd even punch him when he tried to calm me down!' She waits for Richie to interrupt. 'And so I think what happened is that he always took his German calls out of the room, so he didn't frighten me. And I never learnt any of it. My class take French at school,' she finishes, apologetically. 'And next year I'll take Spanish,' she adds, remembering Richie is from Seville.

'You should try to learn while you're here. He will be pleased. It's not good to lose touch. I can help you.'

'I'm not a brilliant learner.'

'I'm not a brilliant teacher.'

Francesca wants to make a joke about her real teachers here, but instead sits smiling back at Richie, who seems pleased to have made this pledge, and to be sitting in this canoe with her, far out on the lake. She reaches forward to take the paddle Richie has balanced in front of him, and catches sight of the bottom of the canoe. They are sitting in a pool of muddy water.

4

Alex arrives at the kiosk first, looks at the handwritten notice and scratches his head. *KEIN EIS.*

Catching him up, Imogen scans the sign and says, 'Never mind, we'll get something else. I'm sure Anja won't mind.'

Alex speaks to the vendor. 'There's another kiosk about ten minutes away, we'll walk to that.'

'In this heat? They'll probably have run out too, and besides, the ice-cream will have melted by the time we get back.'

But Alex has already started walking. 'Ow,' says Imogen, futilely kicking the scalding sand out of her flip-flops.

They walk past other families – raucous settlements, flashes of colour and flesh – and the occasional lone sunbather, in near silence. Imogen thinks how irritating it is when Alex decides he's on a mission. Like there's an emergency and he's going to save the day with lukewarm ice-cream.

After a few minutes, the beach becomes less populated and the golden sand turns into a greyish shingle littered with small rocks. Imogen stubs her toe on one. 'Ow,' she says quietly. Then loudly, for her husband's benefit, 'That hurt. That really hurt.'

Alex pauses for just long enough to smile winningly at Imogen in encouragement. 'We must be almost there.'

'Anja will be wondering where we've got to.'

'She probably thinks we've sneaked back to the house for some alone time.'

'Fat chance,' says Imogen, reaching for Alex's hand companionably.

Alex stops suddenly in the middle of the beach to kiss his wife full on the lips. When he opens his eyes again, there's an old man staring at them. He's carrying an ice-cream cone. 'You see, we're almost there,' says Alex, nodding at the man, who hurries away nervously, stammering to himself in embarrassment.

THE KIOSK HAS a meagre selection of ice-cream, and no containers so everyone has to have their ice-cream in a cone, even though Imogen doesn't like wafer. They've also run out of napkins. The vendor is a jovial man in his sixties, who takes seemingly infinite care in working the ice-cream maker. After the second ice-cream has been handed over, Imogen taps her fingers on the counter in mild exasperation. The man slowly turns from his job. 'Nice day for ice-cream!' he says, smiling widely, showing two prominent gaps in his bottom row of teeth.

Imogen smiles tightly in return, refusing to pick up the snag of conversation.

'WELL, that took forever! These ones were half-melted before he'd even finished making the rest. I told you we should just have got something else from the first kiosk.'

'It's good ice-cream,' Alex replies. 'Have you tried it? It's really good.'

'Anja really will think we've run away.'

'She'll be sunbathing.'

'Oh yes, she'll be sunbathing.'

Alex detects the sarcasm in his wife's voice. He decides to tackle it head on. 'What's up with you two, anyway? You seem – I don't know – cagey with one another.'

'Cagey?'

Don't be drawn into explaining yourself, Alex thinks.

Imogen sighs. 'We're not kids anymore. People change. They have less in common.'

'Especially if they never see each other.'

'Not this again, Alex. We've been busy. We have busy lives, you know that. We're here, aren't we? Damn, it's dripped all down my top. I told you this would be a disaster.'

Alex remembers the last argument before they'd left. Imogen had wanted him to give up the trip, as he had every other time the idea had been raised over the years, but to his surprise he'd found that this time he couldn't. Even if it did mean he was now responsible for what might turn out to be the worst holiday ever.

As they near their original part of the beach, an old man spots them and comes striding towards them, muttering loudly. He's dressed incongruously for the beach, in a buttoned-up suit and tie. To his surprise, Alex recognises the man. I know you, he thinks, but from where? And what could you possibly want with us today?

5

Francesca doesn't immediately know how to tell Richie that the canoe is sinking. It's happening very slowly, a thimble of water at a time, and she is enjoying Richie's easy chatter and her first taste of seclusion with a man who is not her father. Neither is she adept at breaking in when someone else is speaking, even in a matter of comparative urgency. So it is some minutes before a cloud passes and makes Richie think of the shore, and the lunch that awaits them there.

Richie tries to turn the canoe and gain the momentum that had brought them out into the lake. The canoe will not turn.

Francesca opens her mouth to speak. 'There's water—'

'Hang on sweetheart, I'll have us moving in a second.'

'—In the boat. There's water coming in.'

'Just need to pull it round.'

'We're sinking. I should call for help.' The words come out in a rush, and Francesca doesn't know if he's understood. She takes her phone from her pocket, unsure as to whether it will work here, pressing her father's speed dial. Richie sees her action, and puts a hand out to stop her. 'It's okay. I know what to do. Relax.' His touch is warm on Francesca's wrist.

They both watch as Francesca's phone flies through the air, and lands in the lake with a small plop, Francesca grieving immediately for the numbers and messages she has lost.

'What have you done?' she howls, leaning precariously over the water. Why on earth would he knock her phone out of her hand, just when she was trying to help – trying, after all, to save them both from drowning? She glares down at the lake, angry at its indifference when just moments ago the water had seemed to cradle her, keeping her safe. Her breath comes in ragged gasps. If she doesn't do something, she fears she might hyperventilate. Francesca takes three long, deep breaths to calm herself. When she looks up, Richie is smiling sorry into her eyes.

'I'll buy you a new one. Tomorrow. But we don't need to be rescued. We can get out of this on our own. Together.' There are deep etches by his eyes when he smiles. Despite her anger, Francesca would like to draw them.

Of course Richie can't understand what it means for her to lose her phone in this instant. His school year isn't electronically enshrined in a hundred messages and reminders, fragments of abbreviated flirting and poetry with the brevity and complexity of a haiku.

Francesca is not a particularly good swimmer, and ordinarily would not have shown the grit that Richie inspires in her as they both climb out of the canoe, holding on one side each, and begin the slow return to shore, pulling the broken vessel between them. Her grit is really a kind of good grace, as she realises that the one thing Richie does not want is to get into trouble. It's the first time she's noticed this about an adult, and now she doesn't want him to get into trouble either. There is an unspoken agreement between them that if they can make it back to shore without anyone noticing something is amiss, they will simply continue the rest of the day as though nothing has happened, and string the canoe back up where they had found it that morning. The day will be their secret.

So she doesn't allow herself to think about how

deep the water is, and what might lie beneath it. She doesn't complain that the water is really quite cold in some patches, although warmer in others. When they move into busier channels and she accidentally swallows a mouthful of water she recovers as quickly as she humanly can, and grins at the middle-aged couple on a pedalo who would have helped them get back quicker if they'd requested it, to let them know that everything is under control. And actually, it is. There is a constant stream of conversation between the two of them now, punctuated by the irregular splash of Francesca's arm breaking the water. She has given up trying to keep time with Richie, whose single stroke ploughs powerfully and silently on, taking them further with each one of his strokes than she could in five.

'Goofball,' she says, when Richie projects a mouthful of water into the seat of the canoe.

'What is this, golfball?' says Richie, looking confused.

'Yep, you're a golfball alright.'

'Wait! I'm stopping this canoe,' says Richie, shutting down the machine so the pair of them have to tread water while holding on to the vessel. 'You will have to pay!' And Richie reaches over and pushes Francesca's head firmly under the water.

'One.' Deep breath, Francesca is struggling underneath him.

'Two.' Deep breath, this is how Richie settled holiday squabbles with his brothers.

'Three.' Deep breath, Richie relents, untangles his hand from Francesca's wet hair. Francesca comes to the surface, taking great noisy gulps of air.

'I got you,' says Richie, laughing easily.

Francesca says nothing, waiting for her breath to calm, and the feeling that she's about to burst into tears to subside. It's no good, her eyes are stinging; she has to wipe them.

'You're crying!' says Richie, horrified. 'Oh, sweetheart, I didn't mean to make you cry. I'm sorry. I'm sorry again.'

Francesca smiles ruefully through her tears. He hadn't meant to hurt her. He'd probably just forgotten how strong he was. He was just messing around. And somehow she knows, obscurely, that Richie is the sort of person who will get away with most things. He's one of those individuals her mother calls charmed. Of course, it helps that he's beautiful. She can't help but notice *that*. 'It's okay,' she gulps, purposefully starting to pull the canoe along a few more inches, waiting for Richie's strength to propel them onwards.

'LOOK! WE'RE ALMOST BACK,' says Francesca in relief. As she says it, she realises they have another problem. There are a group of people on the shore-line, and they seem to be waving at her and Richie. Her parents are there, and others who seem intent on gaining their attention. As they edge closer to the shore, the canoe zigzagging in first one direction and then the other, Francesca thinks some of the group look angry. She hopes it's just a trick of the sun. Soon, an old man in a brown suit breaks away from the group and walks out into the water, where he attempts to wrestle the canoe from them. Francesca doesn't give the canoe up easily, she can't understand what the man is saying, and her instinct is to hold on for as long as she can. She is ready to bite and kick if she has to.

'Let go, Fran. This is his canoe. It's this man's house we're renting.' Her father has waded into the water up to his knees and taken hold of her to gain her attention. 'We shouldn't have taken the canoe. It's an antique which happens to be worth a great deal of money, and it isn't water-safe. We've been waiting for you to come back.'

'I was going to call the lifeguard, but your father assured me you'd be fine and we should just wait for you to get back. Obviously, you did have problems.' Her mother's gestures are jerky, harbouring an equal measure of relief and annoyance, as unable to move in one direction as the canoe had been when it had started letting in water.

'It was nothing—'

'Serious? People drown, you know. Teenagers drown.'

Francesca looks from her mother to a crestfallen Richie. 'We're fine, mum. I'm fine.'

'And whose idea was it to take the canoe in the first place, Richie? I wondered if you'd have grown up at all, but I guess there's been nothing in your life to make you.'

'Imogen!' Her father's voice is sharp, and Francesca is glad. Her mother had said nothing when the canoe had been brought to the beach. Francesca herself had been the only one who had objected. If only Francesca had stuck to her gut feeling and hadn't let herself be talked around by Richie, none of this would have happened. She thinks how unfair it is that she always seems to get things wrong, even when she starts off in the right.

Francesca's father is trying very hard to smile. He turns to Herr Müller, his hands spread in apology. Francesca decides she should really try to help, to offer an apology to the old man, who suddenly looks vulnerable sweating in his suit in the afternoon sun, but her father waves her down. She isn't to let anything spoil the day. Perhaps she might help Anja with the preparations for lunch.

So Francesca follows her mother through the small crowd back to their spot on the beach, where

Anja is waiting with their belongings. Francesca's face is hot with embarrassment. She turns back to see her father talking animatedly to their landlord, and Richie standing in the water, looking lost. She wishes she could tell Richie her mother's bad mood will pass as suddenly as it had arrived. She'd seen how her mother's comment had hurt him, and thinks it isn't fair – he has no experience of her mother's irrationalities. He'll think she means it.

Anja is sunbathing when they approach, and Francesca sees that she is striking in a different way to any woman she knows at home. Her body is sleekly compact and so tanned that Francesca feels self-conscious sitting down next to her. Anja's long dark hair spills across the beach towel she is spread across and onto the sand. Francesca has always envied curls.

'You were a long time, *na*?'

'Richie took her out in that old canoe from the house. There seems to be a pretty good neighbour-hood-watch system around here, someone must have told the owners. Haven't you seen the fuss?'

Anja shrugs. 'People talk. They all have Handys.'

'Handys?' Francesca is intrigued.

'You know – Handys.' Anja mimes talking on a mobile phone. 'You don't call them that? It's from your language, I thought.'

'It's an imitation of English which isn't as we would use the word, although a lot of German people don't realise that. You'll see it a lot in advertising, Fran. In some cases, the words stick, and seep into common currency.' Imogen smiles at her daughter. For a moment it's as though she's a small child again, and there are so many things she needs Imogen to give her.

'Handy.' Francesca is pleased with her new acquisition.

'I hope you didn't bring yours to the beach with you, Fran. I almost phoned you when you were in the canoe but there's no point you bringing it out at all while we're here.'

Francesca knows she's in trouble. Her mother won't miss a trick, and will be angrier at the loss than Francesca believes is fair – considering it is her birthday present which has been lost, not her mother's, and she has already made her peace with it. Anja saves her by sitting up suddenly, pulling on a tiny white t-shirt and declaring that they must start the barbeque. She asks that Imogen fill up their water supplies while Fran helps her turn their little camp into an eaterie.

After her mother has gone, Anja winks at Francesca and says, 'I'm lucky, I have no-one to nag, not when I'm home from the kindergarten, anyway!'

She doesn't mention Alexandra. It is a name rusted with disuse, from a time that is almost forgotten. She has not spoken it aloud for perhaps nine years.

'I thought we could try that Mexican we used to like tonight.' Imogen has returned, carrying a large bundle of newspapers, as well as the bottles of water Anja requested. 'Just to browse,' she says quietly to her daughter. From a front page, Francesca catches sight of an aeroplane in flames.

'You know what dad'll say,' Francesca replies. 'He thinks she never leaves her desk,' she explains, for Anja's benefit. 'The news is banned when we're on holiday.'

'I can see that could be tricky,' says Anja, neutrally. 'But the restaurant – I don't know if it's still open. I haven't been to that part of the city for many years. Richie and I thought you might like to eat at ours.'

'That's a lovely idea, thank you! But wouldn't it be fun to see a bit of the city? Shall we see what the boys think when they get back?'

'Well, if you—'

'And you'd love the Mexican, Fran – they do the most wonderful ice-cream,' says Imogen to her daughter conspiratorially. Francesca had never got her vanilla cone. 'Don't worry, Anja,' Imogen continues, rummaging for her mobile. 'I'll check whether it's open or not.'

Anja smiles her assent to the change of plan, thinking of the extra expense the night will bring. Richie had told her she wasn't to worry about money while their friends were visiting, but Anja doesn't know how she's supposed to do that.

6

'Look up there, Fran! That was my balcony when I first moved to Berlin. I thought it was wonderful.' Francesca peers up at the grand white building; the balcony her mother is pointing at empty apart from a child's bike. The house next door has its windows missing, and a large sleigh bed is being winched to the ground. Francesca looks at her father questioningly.

'Late 1800s,' he says, 'look at the pattern in the eaves.'

Francesca is proud of her father's ability to date any building, but can do without being reminded of how long and hard he studied for his architecture degree. So can Richie, who always feels fidgety at ostentatious displays of learning.

'Of course, the buildings on this side of the

street pre-date those of the other side by at least a decade. Any ideas how I can tell that, Fran?' He looks at his daughter expectantly. Richie is reminded of a self-important peacock. He always is when Alex starts to talk about buildings. He remembers this even from Alex's student days.

'Well, I'm ready for dinner. I'm starving,' says Richie, saving Francesca from having to answer.

Now that they are here, Imogen would have liked to have spent some more time showing her daughter where she used to live, pointing out the markers of her world back then – the English-language cinema she sometimes had all to herself, the vegetable shop where she was friends with the assistant Maari, the pretty bridge she walked across each day on her way to work – but not even Francesca seems to have much patience for this today. Imogen reasons that they are all tired and hungry, and in Francesca's case, and despite repeated warnings, sunburnt. They'll come back during the week, just the three of them, perhaps with a guidebook, and she'll be able to share her memories with her daughter then.

The Mexican is just around the corner, on another of West Berlin's wide tree-lined streets, its chairs spilling out onto the uneven pavement. If restaurants could hug, that is what Francesca feels as she is welcomed into the warm orange-hued dining space, two waiters fussing over her.

'For you, I have just the table. The perfect spot. For you, I have a very special menu,' says the first waiter, taking her indigo-denim jacket.

'Don't leave your phone or purse in the pocket, Fran,' says her mother, as the waiter disappears.

'They're in my bag,' murmurs Francesca, blushing at the half-lie. She wishes her mum would pay less attention to things, like her best friend Charlotte's mum, who's always losing things and never asks Charlotte where her phone or purse or jewellery is, never tries to link arms with her daughter when crossing the road as Imogen does even now. She should have told her mother about the lost phone right away. She's realised that. Once you're in a lie, it's hard to find a safe exit route, and now she faces the prospect of having to track down the very same model of phone before her mother discovers it's missing, when everyone knows how quickly technology becomes obsolete. Usually, she would have been excited at the prospect of an up-grade – if only her mother were off the case. Still, it isn't all bad. She does have a shopping trip with Richie to look forward to, and despite his klutziness in losing the phone in the first place, Richie seems like someone who could make anything into an adventure. He doesn't really seem like a grown-up at all.

The second waiter, Nico, asks if she's on holiday as he hands her a menu. She's about to reply that she is, when her father cuts in with a torrent of German. Francesca can't understand what her father is saying, and thinks it especially rude for him to do this when the question was hers in the first place.

'He is saying that this is like coming home for you, although you've never been here before,' translates Richie, 'and he has explained that you are half German, although it is something you have not paid much attention to until now.'

'It's my school holiday,' says Francesca, embarrassed at the amount of detail her father has provided.

Nico nods succinctly, and finishes handing out the menus. Francesca catches Richie grinning at himself in the mirror. His reflection winks at her.

FRANCESCA YAWNS. She's been trying to stay interested in the grown-ups' conversation, but all she can do is daydream about the trip Richie has promised her. She watches him talking to her parents and Anja, and she knows that what she is seeing isn't real. The Richie who was alone with her at the lake is different from the man sitting in front of her now. It's as though this is the robotic version of him, and she's the robotic version of herself too. She imagines a whole delicious afternoon alone with the real Richie, perhaps tomorrow.

'It's not like The Green Door here,' says her mother, sniffing.

Francesca is intrigued enough to press pause on her daydream. 'What's The Green Door?'

'The Green Door,' says Anja, leaning forward as though she's got something extremely important to say, 'is where we all first met.'

'Not me,' says Francesca's mother.

'The Green Door,' says Richie, 'was a utopia.'

'The Green Door was an establishment Richie worked in when he first lived in Berlin, almost twenty years ago. It was a café and bar with two options – meat or vegetarian hotpot. The utopian aspect was that people paid whatever they could afford,' says Alex. 'And they had to do it on their way out.'

'Which actually meant The Green Door made a lot of money. Most people didn't ask the rest of their party what they paid, and over-compensated for what they believed the losses were. It was an interesting business model.' Anja wrinkles her nose at the sour taste of her new cocktail.

'The customers brought their own drink. It was a very easy job.' Richie winks across the table at

Fran, but she gets the feeling this won't have been the only reason he worked there. He would have believed in the ideal.

'Were there people who would have gone hungry otherwise?' she asks.

'Some. There was a man called Frank who brought his son in every Saturday. He and his wife had separated and he had moved out of the family home. He never told her he hadn't found anywhere else to go – that he was actually sleeping in the same park where he used to take his son to play football. So, every Saturday, he picked his son up from outside his old house, brought him to eat lunch at The Green Door and pretended everything was normal.'

'And then there were people like Anja,' says Alex. 'She just came because it was trendy.'

'I came because my housemates invited me!'

'You should have met her housemates, Fran. They were the dullest bunch of students the Humboldt can ever have produced. No wonder she found Richie entertaining. He was the real reason she kept coming back.'

'I *was* entertaining,' says Richie, feigning indignation. 'Although I was a little worried that wasn't going to be enough when I left her alone with your father, Fran. I bet you didn't know they grew up in the same district. Or that they went to the same nursery; visited the same bakery.'

'The legendary Oma Hoffman's Bäckerei,' says Anja with a smile. 'Grandma Hoffman frequently sneaked the children an extra pastry when their parents weren't looking, which I always thought I had to keep secret, whereas your father confessed immediately.'

'So you can see which of them is the more honest of the two, can't you, Fran? They also shared a taste for Chinese cinema, and a strong dislike of potatoes.'

Richie doesn't mention that it was only *after* Alex had checked out of life in Germany and cleared out of their flat-share that he and Anja became lovers. The past has a way of confusing even those who lived it.

'And then there was me. I'd grown up in Spain, so no points there. I'd given up on my degree; they were both in their final year when we first met. I also don't have the patience for subtitles, and I am particularly fond of the humble potato, in all of its many incarnations. Although I did always think one of them was exaggerating there.' Richie glances ironically at the empty dish of potato wedges the table had shared. 'What do you think, Fran?'

Francesca doesn't know what to think. 'I'd like an ice-cream,' she says, feeling like a ten-year-old bombarded with things she can't make sense of.

'Well,' says Anja, 'what about all those stories of

you canoeing as a boy? And you didn't know this one was an antique! Perhaps there was a little fabrication in your past, also?'

'Oh no,' says Richie. 'I practically lived on the water. Now—'

'And Alex, what did you say to the owner? He must have taken some sweet-talking. I'm surprised he's letting you stay! Who'd want to rent their property to a family with sticky fingers?'

'A topic for later, I think. Anyway, I thought you were sunbathing!' Francesca notices her father has also begun to look slightly nervous.

'Everybody on that beach knew what was going on. The café's kitchen staff even came out to have a look.'

'Here's Fran's ice-cream. Look, sparklers, sweetheart!' Her father attempts to make room for the ice-cream, shifting the meal's debris into new constellations. Wherever the waiter attempts to place it, Alex blocks him with a new arrangement. Francesca watches the miniature dance in despair.

'Dad! Give me those glasses to hold. I'm sure they can be cleared away now.' She smiles her gratitude at Nico as he takes the glasses from her. He is not much older than she is – he must understand how embarrassingly clumsy fathers can be.

'Every birthday, Fran used to want sparklers. It was more important to her than anything else. We bought her a piano once, but she wasn't happy until she'd had her sparklers!' Her father's grin freezes as he finishes speaking.

Francesca is about to disagree when her mother shushes her and says, 'Alex, stop tormenting your daughter and tell us all what exactly our landlord said.'

Francesca watches her father take a large gulp of Berliner Weiße. He attempts a lofty tone of voice, a bravado that quickly falters. 'He said he needs time to decide whether we can stay or not. We have broken the terms and conditions of our contract and he needs to discuss with his lawyer whether it is a significant breach which would result in our for-feiting our deposit, and the money we have paid up-front for the stay, and having to leave the property.'

For a moment, the sounds of the restaurant fill the gap left after her father has imparted this news. Nico is talking to the barman, who seems to be teaching him how to mix a cocktail. By the window, a family get up to leave. A waitress helps the little girl into the most beautiful white coat, her high-pitched chatter impenetrable to Francesca.

'Hey, it's no problem. You can stay with us. There's plenty of room. Stay with us!' Richie looks from his wife to Imogen. Francesca thinks he really shouldn't have said the words 'no problem' to her mother just then.

Anja wonders if the offer will be good enough this time. It would mean the girl having to sleep in the living room, and after all, their accommodation had been rebuffed the first time around. She shouldn't have been surprised; Imogen has kept her distance over the years. She and Alex have visited at least six European cities in the intervening years by Anja's reckoning, and this is the first time Alex has come home to Berlin. Anja wonders how Imogen managed it. Of course, Alex doesn't have family to pull him back. Anja always felt that was why the bond between Alex and Richie had been so strong; Richie the exchange student continuing to share a flat with Alex even after he had dropped his studies for life at The Green Door. They'd somehow managed to fool the university authorities that Richie was a student long after he should have been back reading psychology at his Spanish university. Anja is grateful to Alex because Richie had once told her that if it hadn't been for Alex, he would have returned to Spain before he and Anja had even had a chance to meet. And if Alex hadn't left Germany – so hurriedly, and so completely – well, there wouldn't have been that vacancy in his house-share for her to fill. She recalls Richie's moping – his lack of belief that his best friend could just disappear with the very barest of communication. It had been all she could do to coax Richie from his bed in those early days. Eventually, she'd realised the only thing to do was to join him in it.

'We don't know what's happening yet, do we? Let's just wait and see what Herr Müller decides before we make any plans. And this time, I shall talk to him myself,' says Imogen, making it clear that Alex obviously hadn't done a very good job earlier despite his long and well-lauded experience in dealing with property. 'Let's just see what happens.'

'Of course,' says Anja, a little too brightly.

7

Francesca wakes early the next morning. She has slept badly, lines from her parents' stifled argument when they returned to the house weaving themselves into her dreams. Her parents had kept drinking long after she'd wanted to leave the restaurant, and she suspects it will be early afternoon before they surface. Richie had said nothing about their shopping trip when they had parted. 'Sleep well, princess,' he said, 'see you soon.' When Francesca was a little girl she'd wished she had the kind of father who called her 'princess' – who thought she was the most perfect girl on the planet. She supposed it was about time that she'd finally met someone who did. Even if he *had* lost her phone and almost drowned her in one day. But what did 'soon' mean? Tomorrow, when I help you find a replacement for the phone I knocked in the water because I thought you were going to tell someone the canoe was sinking; tomorrow when, in turn, I save you from getting into trouble; or some time in the next few days when we all meet up and I've forgotten my promise?

It's hot in the house, and Fran is restless. She tries to ignore her early-morning hunger, as there is little in the kitchen to appease it. Her parents had wasted the milk she would have had on her breakfast cereal on two king-size mugs of coffee on their return last night. Their mugs are still on the kitchen table, three-quarters-full, the liquid cold and discoloured. Francesca is so hungry she briefly considers dowsing the cereal in the cold coffee; instead, she picks a few morsels to eat dry.

Despite her mother's complaint that she has brought too much with her on the trip, Francesca realises she has brought none of the things she really needs. The book of reportage she had been engrossed in – a present from her mother – had been ejected from her bag when, at the last minute, she had carried out a final panicked check for her passport. She can picture the pages shining open on the kitchen floor at home. She hasn't brought her sketchpad or any of her drawing materials. Her phone provided her with music so she'd decided not to bring her iPod. And now the phone is at the bottom of the lake she has no music to listen to or games to play. In one way this is a good thing – she'd been fighting an addiction to one of the games on her phone. Now she'll have to undergo an unavoidable period of cold turkey.

With nothing to do, and no idea when her parents will wake, the hour moves excruciatingly slowly. The only means of keeping time is a large white clock in the kitchen that's marked with roman numerals. Francesca studies it closely, convinced it is taking a tiny jump backwards every six seconds.

She thinks of all the things she could be doing were she at home, and then of the vast city she is in. It's true that she hasn't spent a lot of time thinking about her father's country. She remembers the book he left on her bed at home. 'To research the trip,' he said. But Francesca hadn't been able to get past the dull introduction, which went right back to the country's origins in Ancient Rome.

Last night she had begun to hear snippets of her parents' life together in Berlin, had begun to piece together the names of the different districts as her parents had known them. Tiergarten, Charlottenburg, Kreuzberg. Richie explained that where there had then been twenty-three separate districts there were now twelve, but that many people still used the old names. Francesca has found she is terrified of forgetting anything Richie tells her. It's as though each morsel of information is entrusted to her for safekeeping, and at any moment he might ask for it back again.

It is too much that her parents are sleeping when there is a city to see. Francesca begins to feel like a caged animal, padding quietly through a too-small domain, prowling for something – anything – to hold her attention. They may not wake for hours. Francesca weighs up what her mother would have said had she asked her permission to explore the city on her own, knowing she would probably have pointed out that Francesca has not been out enough to get her bearings, and that she does not even know the language well enough to help her find her way. But of course she may also take into account Francesca's new-found sense of responsibility, her undeniable maturity. She could offer a pleasant surprise. Smiling at the thought, and in gracious acceptance of the new freedoms being given to her, Francesca pulls the front door closed with a soft click.

FRANCESCA WALKS past a dozen houses like theirs, houses in which everyone seems to be asleep. Large, spacious houses with a variety of vehicles for land and water waiting like additional limbs in the driveways. She feels a shiver of excitement at the vastness of the city, and her part in it. It's as though she's the only person awake in the whole of Berlin. She touches a part of each property with her toes as she passes, fulfilling an imaginary mission to bring the city into consciousness. She has reached the tram-line before she thinks she should have left a note for her parents.

'We just need to be reassured you're safe, that's all.' She remembers her mother's words the day she had returned from the television studio after news had broken that a local boy had gone missing whilst camping in the Scottish Highlands with his family. Francesca hadn't been watching the news, and hadn't taken her mother's plea seriously until a week later, when the boy still hadn't returned. They made jokes about it at school. The stupidest ways he could have died. The jokes mostly centred on the boy having left his tent in the night to go to the toilet. Some people, Francesca included, thought he'd been kidnapped and smuggled abroad to join the new slave trade. She'd seen a documentary about it online once, the kind of thing her mother hates her watching.

She should really have left a note, she thinks, as she boards a tram marked 'Mariendorf'. She decides to ride the tram to the end of the line and then back again, before her parents have even noticed she's gone.

A morning mist has descended, so Francesca's sightseeing is somewhat limited. She doesn't notice it is the end of the line until the driver coughs twice and waves his hand towards the door.

Outside, there is a lone bench opposite a short promenade of shops. It's drizzling, and the only shop open is a bakery, where Francesca buys a hot slice of sweet apple strudel to savour while she waits for the returning tram. She has a single two Euro coin left to pay for the journey.

'You are Polish?'

Francesca turns to see an oddly-dressed man smiling at her.

She shakes her head slightly and looks away – a polite signal that she will not be drawn into conversation.

'There's no harm in talking, baby. I only asked where you are from.'

Francesca smiles nervously. She concentrates on her fingernails, bitten so compulsively she does not even notice she is doing it anymore; her embroidered bag, with its sweet wrappers, bus tickets and trio of lost lip-balm lids. She holds her coin warm in her palm of her hand.

'It's a lonely world today, baby, when you can't ask a pretty girl where she's from.' There is a hint of hysteria in the stranger's voice.

'I'm not Polish,' mumbles Francesca, hoping that

will be an end to the conversation, and the man will leave her alone. He moves closer. 'Ah – you are Canadian? Or Australian? Or Irish, pretty baby?' There's a glint in the man's eye as he attempts a strained Irish lilt, and Francesca sees that he's playing with her, and she doesn't know the rules. She shakes her head again, wishing there is someone else around.

'What do you say, baby?'

Francesca coughs, wanting to be away. 'None of those,' she shrugs, trying to appear nonchalant, in control. She holds her identity close to her, not wanting to give any of it away. The man is quiet, waiting. He moves to scan the peeling timetable behind her – then in a sudden movement that reminds her of a wild cat she'd once seen land next to its prey, takes a seat beside her.

Francesca is torn. It seems so very rude to stand because the man has chosen to sit – it is, after all, a public bench and she has no more right to it than he.

The yellow bench has silver armrests separating it into three. Somehow, though, the man oozes into her seat too. His physical presence is unignorable. She can feel his breathing, his heat. It looks as though he spilt his breakfast on his jeans, and there's a gap where the denim doesn't quite meet his socks. When he swings one leg to cross over the other, she can see the thick black hairs on his shin.

Oh, why couldn't he choose the seat at the end, she thinks in frustration, scuffing her foot against the ground. She would be able to bear that. But now the need to move is building up in her; she can't stay with his foot tapping impatiently a millisecond from hers.

Francesca shivers and gets up from the bench. As she crosses the road towards the bakery, the man follows. 'Wait. I just want to talk to you, baby!' He is still behind her, matching his pace to hers. As she approaches the bakery she can see that it too is closed now. Francesca breaks into a run. The man's footsteps echo hers. 'Wait, baby. Wait!' he calls after her insistently. 'You don't need to be frightened.' Francesca takes turning after turning, muddling left with right until she has no idea how to get back to the tramline anymore. Each road is unfamiliar, but when she listens she hears the familiar tread of the man following her, calling 'Wait, baby. Wait!'

8

As Francesca runs she realises she has crossed into a poor area of the city, full of cheap chain-stores and vandalised phone boxes. The drizzle has turned to great drops of rain. Francesca has never noticed rain make such a noise before. It batters down relentlessly, bouncing high off the pavement.

Her mouth aches and her jeans are heavy from the rain, her silver trainers filthy from being dragged through the waterlogged streets. She stumbles, falls. She's scraped her knee and it feels like it's bleeding, but there's no time to check. Her single coin has slipped out of her hand and is nowhere to be seen.

Francesca scrambles to her feet and forces herself to carry on running down the wide and desolate road. The shops all seem to be shut, and there is no one she can ask for help.

Francesca wonders whether it is possible to become more lost the further she runs. Or is there a finite state of being lost, a point at which someone is as lost as they'll ever be? She wonders if anyone has worked out the probability of becoming more or less lost the further you go, like they have with what you should do if you arrive at a bus stop with no idea when the next bus will come. She tries to think how the probability could be calculated. It is a displacement activity. She daren't think what will happen if the man catches up with her, or how angry her parents will be when she finally gets home.

And then suddenly, looming right in front of her as if from nowhere is a shop with its lights on. Francesca carries right on running, through the doors with their peeling orange paint, leaving them banging shut behind her. She stops at the counter, where a boy of about nineteen, wearing dungarees and a baseball cap, is standing. He seems to instinctively know what he needs to do, as he hurries outside, throwing his big booming voice into a volley of shouts.

As Francesca waits inside for her panic to die down, she realises it isn't a shop at all that she's standing in, but a small bar with a darts board, and a few bottles lined up on a dusty-looking shelf. Only now does she notice the four customers that are all drinking a clear liquid that is specked with gold. They don't speak to her. The only sounds are Francesca's ragged breath and the barman's cries outside.

Finally, the barman returns, saying something Francesca can't understand.

'There was a man,' Francesca says. 'A man following me.'

'Ah, English,' grins the young man, touching his grubby baseball cap. 'Don't worry. I see him off!'

He motions for Francesca to stay where she is, and disappears again, this time into the back of the bar.

He returns, holds his hand out for Francesca to shake, and presents her with the empty glass, which she holds steady while he fills it with a generous measure of the gold-speckled spirit. He motions for Francesca to wait while he collects his own glass.

'*Prost,*' says the barman, knocking his glass against hers in toast.

'I'm sorry, I don't have any money,' says Francesca, smiling apologetically.

'It is a gift,' he replies, smiling broadly and tugging at his baseball cap before leading Francesca over to the other drinkers, who line up their shot glasses expectantly. He fills each glass in one fluid movement, and an elaborate ritual begins whereby each drinker locks eyes with each of the others in turn, sharing the toast with every member of the group before the drinking can commence.

Fran drinks the shot of liquid in one go, as she has watched the others do. It burns her stomach and she forgets the trouble she is in.

'Again?' asks the barman.

Francesca nods giddily.

HALF AN HOUR LATER, Francesca is happily playing cards with her new friends. Antonio has introduced her to everyone, and she has come to realise that though she thought she had stumbled into a public bar, everyone here is related in some way, or old school-friends of Antonio. It is as far from the idea of a 'public house' as is possible. The bar is also severely under-stocked, and seems to operate within a very loose business frame. Seeing Antonio wave away yet another offer of payment, Francesca asks him if his boss will be angry when he sees how much money has been made today. Antonio looks perplexed.

'These are my friends, my family,' he says. 'My uncle didn't buy this bar to make money. And anyway, Mikey here will pick me up some things I want when he goes to Poland tomorrow. My uncle too.'

The idea goes against everything Francesca has been taught.

'But you gave me a drink for free before I even sat down. I have nothing to pay you with and nothing I can give you in exchange.'

'You give me English lessons. I have to pass my English exam for my apprenticeship. That is your gift. Now, play!' He waits for Francesca to reveal her final card.

THE USUAL FORFEIT for losing at cards in Antonio's bar involves partial nudity and the darts board. Nobody has mentioned this to Francesca, and when Francesca loses, Antonio turns to her and says, 'what are you doing out on your own anyway? I bet you've got the kind of family that wouldn't want you drinking Goldschlager at one o-clock on a Sunday afternoon.'

'It's one already? I'm dead!' Francesca explains how she had gotten lost – and that she has to get back to their house by the lake, but she's not sure exactly where it is or even which tram stop she got on at that morning. Antonio grins – he is used to sorting out people's problems. He takes a pen from behind the bar, and begins drawing a large map across four beer-mats.

'Did you pass a supermarket?'

'What kind of street lighting did you notice?'

'Was there a special crossing to let you get over the tramlines?'

Francesca feels useless – she really hadn't noticed much at all. Antonio drills her relentlessly and she remembers nothing of any use. Until she recalls a box – a large blue metal box, its outline lurking at the very edge of her consciousness. She'd wondered what it was for, and then forgotten she'd ever wondered at all.

'A generator!'

And before Francesca has caught up, Antonio is leading a heated discussion with the rest of the bar. Each of Antonio's friends has a passionate opinion on the whereabouts of the tram stop, but it is Jan, a softly spoken courier with a long beard, who finally solves the puzzle. Stepping forward into the middle of the bar, Jan has to resort to waving his arms to quieten the din of the other three drinkers to make his announcement.

'There is only one blue generator near Wannsee, and it is here!' Jan croaks triumphantly, marking an 'x' on his beer-mat map.

Antonio knocks three times on the table and announces he is closing the bar for lunch. 'Can't have you wandering the city lost. Who knows what damage you could do!' he says to Francesca's protests.

WITH ANTONIO AS HER GUIDE, it isn't long before Francesca begins to recognise some of the roads they are on. 'You really ran round in circles!' he says when she describes the morning's journey. He teaches her how to ask for two one-way tickets when they get to the tram. 'With confidence!' he shouts when she gets it wrong, leaving Francesca crying with laughter.

'*Einzelfahrt bitte. Zwei—*'

'"*Zwo*" – we are from east Berlin! Like this – "*Zwo.*"'

'*Zwo. Einzelfahrt bitte.*' Antonio applauds and the driver gestures for them to move up into the carriage. The rain has cleared and on this journey Francesca is determined not to let anything escape her attention.

STANDING at the end of a street with the blue generator, Antonio tells Francesca to wait while he draws a more detailed map, showing her how to use it to get back to the bar.

'*Die Lustige Riesen*,' Francesca reads from above a

large cross. 'The happy ... raisin? Is that what your uncle's bar's called, Antonio? The happy raisin!'

'De Loostige Riesen,' corrects Antonio. 'The Riesen is like a big man, a too big man. He scares everybody but it's not his fault. Like – Jack and the Beanstalk.'

'You mean a giant? So it's "The Happy Giant?"'

'De loostige Riesen,' she repeats, pleased to add another strange new phrase to her collection. She's picking up new words all the time now, and to her amazement, they seem to be sticking. 'It must be because I'm half German,' she thinks with a stab of pride. She's always found learning new vocabulary for French at school impossible – a pile of empty words she has no use for – and had assumed she'd never be a linguist. Her French teacher would choke if she saw her.

Antonio takes out his phone, checking it rapidly and writing his number across the front of the map in large, deliberate digits. There will be a party for his sister Ingrid's birthday, he explains.

'But I won't be able to call,' Francesca says, her smile clouding. 'I dropped my phone in the lake.'

'Tsk,' says Antonio, reaching into the depths of his coat, and bringing out a second phone. 'You can borrow this one. Just be careful with it. Don't let it go swimming,' he grins. Then he bends to give

Francesca a sudden hug goodbye, making her promise to call him if she gets lost again.

Francesca watches him walk away, tall and clumsy and out of place in this neighbourhood with its well-tended gardens and super-size driveways.

9

'Your mother tried to make a friend of Herr Müller. Evidently a Sunday is not the day to befriend Herr Müller,' says Francesca's father in explanation of why their three suitcases are waiting on the lawn when Francesca returns.

'That's another no go. I can't believe it. A city the size of this and all the suitable accommodation has gone,' shouts her mother through the open window.

'I told you an hour ago – there's a parade on!'

'Oh yes, a parade! Will that fill all the accommodation in the entire city?'

'We already have a perfectly good invitation. I don't know why you can't just let me ring Richie.'

'I've another number to try first. And I've a good feeling about this one—'

'Anja will wonder why we don't want to stay with them. They want to help, you know.'

'I know they do, darling – but will they really want us to all be cooped up together? That tiny flat was fine when we were all in our twenties but I'm not sure I could bear it now. Let me just try this last one.'

'Well, you can call our friends afterwards whatever the outcome is. We haven't got long, you know – Herr Müller will be here soon to conduct a full itinerary and collect his keys. And don't forget Richie's birthday. We'll have to get a present.'

Fantastic, thinks Francesca, making herself comfortable on Herr Müller's sun lounger and daydreaming about a gift for Richie – her parents have hardly noticed she was missing.

'We tried to call you actually, Fran – where've you been and why don't you have your phoned switched on? We were getting worried.' Francesca is infinitely glad it is her father who gets in first with these questions. Her parents must have slept as late as she had thought they would, and then been too busy packing and frantically trying to find a hotel to attempt to track her down.

'I just had a walk down to the lake – it seemed a shame to ruin the peace and quiet by bringing my phone with me.' Francesca knows her father isn't a fan of modern technology – he can leave his own phone uncharged for weeks. He saves all the news-paper articles which point to the various risks of the new technology – lower fertility, the possibility of throat cancer – and takes them to her school parents' evenings to try and persuade the school to ban mobile phones anywhere on the school grounds. He would also like to outlaw wireless internet connections. It is a uniquely embarrassing foible for Fran to deal with, but it does mean he doesn't believe in teenage sur-veillance to quite the extent her mother does.

'What on earth happened to your clothes, Fran? They're filthy.' Her mother has homed in on her through the kitchen window.

'I was at the lake...' says Francesca, squirming.

'Well, you won't have time to get changed now. Herr Müller will be here any minute. You'll have to shower at Anja and Richie's. And you can't come back in here traipsing mud either – I've just mopped the floor.'

'What about all my stuff?'

'Your father packed for you. And don't let's hear about your precious privacy rights – it was an emer-gency, and he won't have looked at anything anyway. Although of course, we do have nothing better to do than snoop on you.'

'Did you get my green sandals from the cup-board? And my new t-shirt from my ensuite?'

Francesca asks her father, trying not to picture him having to retrieve her dirty underwear from the floor. She makes a mental note to be less of a slob at Richie and Anja's.

'It's all taken care of,' says Alex, lobbing a tennis ball in her direction. Francesca watches it whizz past her head and drop over the neighbour's fence. 'You were supposed to intersect it!' he says father, shaking his head. 'You know, jump!'

'Sorry,' says Francesca, smiling ruefully. 'Shall I go round and get it?'

'No time,' says her father, nodding at the red Mercedes that has just pulled up outside the house. 'I doubt he'll miss a tennis ball anyway,' he murmurs, striding to greet their soon-to-be-ex-landlord as he emerges from the car.

FROM THE FRONT of the taxi, Imogen breaks the silence. 'Well, *that* was embarrassing.' She doesn't turn to look at Alex as she speaks, and Francesca thinks it must be very strange to be a taxi-driver sometimes. To know when you're wanted in a conversation or out of it; when you're supposed to be present, and when you're meant to be invisible. If Francesca were a taxi-driver, she'd find it hard not to show she were listening to other people's conversations. She could imagine herself laughing out loud, or butting in with her own opinions.

'Nonsense. It was an honest mistake. The man didn't have a heart, or a sense of humour either.'

'It was all written down in the welcome pack. How the canoe was a family heirloom and guests aren't to touch it. You told me you'd read everything.'

'How else was I supposed to get you to relax?'

'And you wonder why I want to check things...'

Francesca listens to her mother's words move up a pitch and thinks that maybe she's like the taxi-driver after all. She's used to knowing when something doesn't concern her; when her opinion wouldn't be welcome. She most definitely knows not to interrupt her parents when they're arguing. If Francesca could, she'd stick up for her father, but then she can usually see her mother's point of view too. It's true, for instance, that her dad's always getting things wrong, things her mother would have checked.

Outside, the streets are beginning to fill up for the parade. Lines of people in extravagant costumes straggle slowly across the road. The taxi-driver beeps at a group that almost don't get out of his way quickly enough. Francesca watches the back of his head shaking in annoyance. There's a man on stilts, and someone in a giant spider costume. People are linking arms, or holding hands with someone and no matter how slowly they are moving and how much it is infuriating the taxi-driver, everyone seems to be taking part in a dance, as if they are all invisibly linked.

The taxi-driver winds his window down a few inches, and a blast of music fills the car. Samba. He spits a ball of chewing gum out of the window and winds it up again.

There is silence until the car pulls up outside a tall block of flats and the driver looks round at Alex.

'Are you sure we're in the right place?' Imogen asks. 'This doesn't look right.'

'Mommsenstraße?' asks Alex, checking the address with the driver. The driver smiles, nods, and holds his hand out. Alex shrugs and counts four notes.

'Talk to him, Alex. I don't think this is right,' says Imogen, poking Alex in the shoulder.

'He says this is the stop for Mommsenstraße. "Everybody out," he says. Perhaps it's not far for us to walk from here. I'll get my bearings once I'm outside.'

'Everybody out,' says the taxi-driver in English, smiling jovially as though he's made a joke. 'Boot open,' he adds. 'Not shoe, boot. Ha ha.'

'Get the suitcases out, will you Fran,' says Alex.

'Don't get Fran to do it,' huffs Imogen. 'He might run her over.'

'Run her over!' wheezes the taxi-driver, making running movements with his fingers.

'WELL, this is *a* Mommsenstraße, just not *the* Mommsenstraße,' says Alex, staring up at a sign fixed to the graffiti-stained wall. *THE STASI LIVES* is written in large pink letters; at Alex's head is a red target with the words *YOU ARE HERE*. Across the top of the building there is a picture of two cars crashing, and the date 10.08.87.

'Fantastic, Alex. I could have told you it wasn't *the* street back in the taxi.'

'I think we would have been forcibly evicted if we hadn't got out when we did. The driver was a fruitcake.'

Francesca is sitting on her suitcase, while her parents walk up and down shouting at each another. A young woman appears at the window of one of the flats and looks out at them. She's nursing a red-faced baby, and when she stops Francesca can see the baby is about to cry. In the distance, Francesca can hear the slowed beat of the Samba. She longs to join in, to follow the flashes of colour she'd seen from the car.

'I'm hungry, mum,' says Francesca, hoping this

will encourage her parents to move, or at least start making a plan.

'In a minute, Fran!' they both say at once, and Francesca thinks she can see the beginnings of a smile on her mother's lips.

'How about some mint Ritter?' Imogen says, relenting. She fishes in her bag for the half bar of chocolate she's been saving and divides it into three portions, handing the larger two to her husband and daughter. Imogen humps her laptop-bag over her shoulder, takes hold of two of the suitcases and starts walking. 'Come on then!' she says over her shoulder, like a tour guide rounding up two flagging tourists.

Fran follows behind her father; there's a tug at her heart as she realises they're heading away from the parade.

WHEN THE SECOND taxi pulls up outside the second Mommsenstraße, Richie bounds out to greet the family.

'We thought you'd gotten lost,' he says, folding Alex into a giant hug.

'We did,' says Imogen, offering Richie her cheek.

'I thought you knew this place, Alex!' says Richie, squeezing Francesca's hand. 'Let me take your bag, *Liebchen*. Anja's been getting everything ready. We're so excited you're coming to stay. I think Anja hoped you'd stay all along. It'll be just like it used to be!'

Except for me and the fish, thinks Francesca as she hurries to follow her parents and Richie into the house before the door swings shut behind them. This time, she notices that the walls are painted a bright yellow and that on the wall next to each of the doors leading to the separate flats small flower baskets are fixed. The first one they pass has near-skeletal plants, obviously long-neglected. The second is empty, but in the third a vibrant mixture of purple and red pansies is on proud display. There's no flower basket outside the door of Richie and Anja's flat, right at the top of the building, but in a small window looking out from the top of the kitchen into the hallway is the stark silhouette of a single white orchid.

Francesca peers into the white wicker basket of a small child's bike across the hallway as they wait for Anja to come to the door. A half-peeled satsuma, a schoolbook covered in stickers, an unopened carton of juice. The carton has a picture of an orange but with the word *Apfelsine* printed over it, which Francesca finds confusing. She's sure *Apfel* means apple.

Anja comes to the door, wearing a green spotted apron over a short chiffon dress. Her hair is pinned up elegantly today, with two or three curls carefully framing her face. 'Come in! I've made gazpacho,' she says, leading the way through a small dark hallway into the lounge, where the table is set for five. As Francesca follows, she sees Anja's hair is held in place by a silver butterfly. It's the most beautiful accessory Francesca has ever seen, and she wants one badly. Francesca wonders if she might get to go shopping with Anja while she's here. It'll have to be when her mother can't come – her mother's too sensible, never encourages her to try anything too glamorous or pretty or showy. Perhaps her mother will get one of her headaches, and Anja will offer to take Francesca out. That's the only way it would work – Francesca would never want to offend her mother.

'This looks delicious, Anja. And everything's so homely. You'll have to teach me to cook while I'm here. And madam, too. Fran's about as useless in the kitchen as I am, I'm afraid.' Imogen has chosen a seat with her back to the fish-tank. It's a tight squeeze, and Francesca bets she wishes she hadn't been so quick to sit down. The soup's cold, after all.

'We're so glad you're here,' says Anja, serving the soup into pretty porcelain bowls and daintily dropping little swirls of pesto sauce on top.

'Delicious,' says Alex, scooping up a handful of freshly-made croutons.

'So,' says Richie, grinning, 'tell us what happened with the landlord.'

'That orchid is beautiful, Anja,' Imogen says quickly, before Alex can reply. 'I didn't notice it before.'

'Be sure to make yourself at home,' says Anja, breezily. 'I'll be leaving for work before you'll be getting up probably, but Richie will take care of you.'

'At the kindergarten?' asks Fran. She can't keep the note of excitement from her voice.

'Of course.' Anja seems to weigh something up. 'You can come if you want,' she suggests tentatively, as though sure Francesca will decline.

'Could I! Could I really?' Francesca asks, looking first at Anja and then at her mother.

'Yes, our English assistant is on holiday. You can play some games with the older children.'

'You don't have to, Fran. Your father and I will be sightseeing—'

Francesca thinks that her mother sounds flustered, panicked.

'Well, no, if Fran would like to see something of the working world, of course that would be fine. It's a very kind offer.'

Francesca beams, thankful that her father has at least managed to cut off her mother's rudeness, if not obscure it entirely. She doesn't remember her mum ever being this rude to someone. No one else seems to have noticed, though – the conversation appears to be moving on as normal. Perhaps Anja will even take her shopping after the kindergarten is over. This reminds Francesca of Richie's promise, but suddenly that doesn't seem so important anymore. What will really happen to her if her mother realises she's lost her phone, and what could ever really happen between her and Richie anyway? And just like that, Francesca drowns the idea of her day with The Real Richie at the bottom of the lake, where it comes to rest next to her orange mobile phone.

'You don't have to go with Anja, Fran. Not if you don't want to.' Francesca thought her mother had whispered this almost hopefully, catching Francesca on her own in the hallway later that evening. Her mother must have waited for the right moment, to make it seem natural that she was giving Francesca a chance to back out of spending a day at the kindergarten with Anja. Letting her daughter know that it wouldn't matter, that she would smooth over any hurt feelings or ruffled feathers. It was quite strange really, and not the sort of thing Francesca's mother would usually have worried about. Perhaps it's the menopause, and she's missing her work in the studio, thinks Francesca. Perhaps that's making her mother jealous, and she's worried Francesca's going to prefer spending time with Anja than with her. Whilst Anja is definitely more glamorous than her practical and hardworking mother, Francesca hopes her mother doesn't really think she's that fickle. It's not like she's totally comfortable with Anja, anyway. Francesca gets the feeling that Anja's always weighing up her words, working out how much she can say, what she *should* say.

Take this morning, walking to the kindergarten together. Francesca had wanted to hear a little about her mother's life in Berlin. She'd begun to ask a question, saying, 'you were friends with my mother before she met my father, weren't you?' but Anja had umm-ed and ahh-ed like she was facing an accusation. She didn't want to talk about it. Francesca understands what that's like – she's always being asked things she doesn't want to disclose. Usually because she's broken some rule or other. She's too young to enter a pub (unless it's with her parents and they're eating there). She's too young to have boyfriends more than two years older than her (a ridiculous rule). She's too young to get any part of her body pierced except her ears (where, if she chose, she could have up to three holes in each ear). While she's actually only broken one of these rules (by drinking in Antonio's bar), there seems to be an infinite number of things a fourteen-year-old can get wrong on a daily basis, and

Francesca often feels like she's on the cusp of giving too much away, of implicating herself for something she hasn't even thought of, let alone done. The worst had been one time in assembly at school, when someone had vandalised the girls' toilets. The deputy headmistress, a small lady with tidy grey hair who Francesca had always got along with because she was good at art, had quietly described how 'disappointed and distressed' she had been to learn that one of her own pupils was responsible for such mindless destruction. Even though Francesca had never even scored her name onto a school desk, let alone smashed through the separating walls of the toilet cubicles and smeared the doors with faeces, the deputy headmistress's words had gnawed at her conscience. First Francesca's head had flushed, then her whole body. The heat had been insufferable. She'd felt she'd have to confess or faint.

So Francesca knows about guilt, both real and imagined. She knows it's possible to take on someone else's guilt as easily as catching a virus.

MAX AND MORITZ is a private kindergarten where all the children have two hours of English in the morning and the elder children have an additional hour of French in the afternoon. Fifteen years ago,

Francesca's mother had been one of the teachers of English.

'Is it really the same?' Francesca asks Anja as they walk through the reception hall, decorated with children's posters proclaiming 'welcome' in nine different languages. 'The same as when mum worked here?'

'Those posters are different. The walls are the same, though. They need painting.' Anja nods at the caretaker as they pass the gym.

Apart from the caretaker, Anja and Francesca seem to be the first in the building, the sound of Anja's stiletto heels clacking sharply through the corridor. Anja's classroom is the last one on the central corridor. It's also the largest, and the only one with a view of the school's garden. As the class teacher who has been there the longest, Anja long ago manoeuvred herself into the best position.

'Wow! Look at all this,' says Francesca, going straight to the corner where what seems like hundreds of children's books and games are stacked. She takes out a giant book of pop-up fairytales and sits on a little red chair at a tiny table to read it.

'I'd forgotten some of these,' she says, turning to the story of Thumbelina. 'This was one of my favourites. I'd get dad to read it to me every single day, sometimes twice!'

'Our little girl liked that one too.' Anja speaks

without thinking. It's the shock of recognising a detail long forgotten. Their little girl had liked to listen to a tape of *Thumbelina* while she was getting dressed in the morning.

'You've got a daughter?'

'She died. She would have been eight months younger than you.'

'Oh.' Francesca doesn't know what to say. She's never talked about death so directly; doesn't think to offer condolences; it's not a situation she's been in before. She wants to ask questions. When did it happen? How old was she when she died? What was she called? How did she die? Did she look more like you or Richie? Do you think we'd have been friends?

'Geronimooooooo.' A small sandy-haired boy bursts into the room with his arms outstretched, pretending to fly in a circle around the room. He comes to a halt in front of Francesca.

'Who are *you*?' he asks, wiping his nose with his hand.

'This is Francesca, Thomas. She's going to be helping you with your English today,' says Anja.

'You're little,' says Thomas, returning to his friends who are with their parents in the corridor, exchanging their outside shoes for the soft indoor ones they wear each day at the kindergarten. 'We've got a new English teacher, and she's LITTLE,' he tells his classmates with authority.

Anja chats with the parents for a few minutes before chivvying the children into the classroom. There's a mixture of ages, from toddlers to grown-up-looking six year-olds. Anja gathers them all round to introduce Francesca, explaining emphatically that Francesca can't speak a word of German, so any communication with her will have to be in English. 'If we tell them that you'll be surprised by what they come out with. Nothing teaches better than necessity,' Anja matter-of-factly explains to Francesca while the children are busy setting the tables with plastic cloths and handing round cut-out fishes.

As FRANCESCA SITS APART from the class, she watches Anja dealing with the little children and thinks again of her mother. It's hard to imagine her here. Francesca has been to her mother's work on several occasions – when she was little; when she's been sick; and once, when she was eleven, she even shadowed her for a whole day in a special school project.

She remembers writing the school report the next day, how she'd made sure everyone would understand how powerful and important her mother

was at work. *Her* mother was the one who put together the news programmes everyone else's parents watched. She knew that was special – more
special than working in a bank, say, or working part-
time in a florist's, like Charlotte's mum. More special
than being a housewife, or a school-teacher.

The class English teacher had been in charge of
picking who would get to read their report to the
whole year, and Francesca had desperately wanted
to be chosen. But from her class, Mrs Mitchell had
picked Robin, whose father was a tree surgeon, and
Amelia, whose mother made chocolates. Francesca
couldn't believe how either of those could be more
vital to the daily business of life than a news editor
and had ended the day fighting with Robin in the
playground while the rest of her class cheered
him on.

Observing Anja today, though, what Francesca
really remembers from that day is how quick everything had been. Her mother had had so many decisions to make, so many tasks to do, and so many
orders to give to her assistants, that she'd barely had
time to explain anything to Francesca. 'Just watch,'
she'd instructed at the beginning of the day, and
that was exactly what Francesca had done. There
hadn't been time for any questions that evening either – it had been such a stressful day that her
mother had come home to order dinner, bath, and

bed – so much of Francesca's report had been a loose interpretation of what she'd thought had been going on in offices she hadn't visited, and the explanations she thought *might* fit tasks she hadn't understood.

So it's hard to imagine her mother slowing to the speed of sixteen kindergarten children, helping them with sequins and paints and glue as Anja does with an armour of indestructible calm. Francesca wonders what her mother would be like if she'd stayed here for all those years, as Anja has done. That's weird, of course, because it means she, Francesca, would have been brought up in Germany, like these children. She'd be a completely different person. The British side of her personality would be the one that would be hidden, the side that would be submerged. How strange that would be. There's no way the two sides could ever be balanced – unless she spent half of every year in one country, and half in the other. But she'd have to rotate the seasons too – it wouldn't seem fair to always spend Christmas or summer in the same country, so it would have to go in a strange pattern, a bit like crop rotation. It makes her head spin just to think about it.

FRANCESCA HELPS each child glue a bamboo stick to

the back of their fish, so they each have their own puppet.

'Now,' Anja says, disappearing to fetch a large cardboard frame from the cupboard. 'It's time to tell Francesca the story of The Little Fish Who Thought He Was Lunch.'

Thomas sticks his hand up urgently, as though there's an emergency in the room. 'Miss! Miss! What about the seaweed, Miss?'

Anja disappears inside one of the cupboards camouflaged by the children's artwork at the back of the room. 'Here it is,' she says, fixing the cardboard seaweed to the bottom of the frame.

Francesca watches as Anja splits the children into two groups and explains their part in the story. Most of the children are part of a shoal of large fishes but a little boy with glowing eyes has been intricately decorating a much smaller one.

Francesca sits on a beanbag and watches as the tale of Dominic's little fish unfolds in front of her.

It's a sweet story. One small fish is scared of another large fish that always leaves its shoal to look for him at lunch-time. Francesca laughs as the children all wave their shiny multi-coloured fishes at her. Dani's fish with the purple tail chases Dominic's round in circles. Dani's ponytail is bobbing furiously above the seaweed.

Dominic's little fish thinks Dani's big fish wants

to eat him. The large fish tries to talk to him but the little fish always swims away, terrified. 'Go, Dominic, go!' hisses Dani from behind the scenery.

One day the large fish catches the little fish and the little fish is terrified. This is it, he thinks. He's about to be eaten. The big fish takes the little fish back to his house, where the table is set for dinner. (Two cardboard plates are lowered trembling into position.) The little fish quakes, and Dominic shakes his body for all he's worth. But the large fish busies himself getting the table set for his smaller friend. He wants to invite him to lunch!

'You understand?' asks Dortje, appearing at Francesca's side. 'The little fish didn't need to be so frightened. The big fish only wanted to share his lunch with him.'

'It's a nice story,' says Francesca, wondering if she should add that sometimes you do have to be careful. She thinks of the man following her through the streets yesterday. Why did he want to catch up with her so badly? Dortje is looking up at her enquiringly. 'It's a nice story,' Francesca repeats. 'Sometimes people just want to be friends and for some reason we don't see it. And if we're scared all the time we won't make any friends at all.' Dortje's only five, after all. And anyway, there *had* been Antonio. He hadn't wanted anything from her; he'd gone out of his way to make sure she was okay. He saved her from being lost and presented her with an expensive mobile phone without asking anything in return, even though Francesca suspects he doesn't have much money himself. And Antonio isn't like anyone else Francesca has known; ordinarily their paths would never have crossed.

AFTER LUNCH, Francesca plays a board game with Dortje, Dani, Thomas and Sam. Sam's a pale little boy with a cold. He's a very competitive child, in a different way to Dani. Whereas Dani is happy as long as she's let everyone know she's boss, Sam is possessed with a desperate desire to win every round. It's a game to test the children's English vocabulary, and Francesca tries to let the children have an equal number of attempts at answering the questions, but Sam is always ready to blurt out an answer, even when it's not his go. When he finally gets an answer wrong, Francesca shushes him and asks Dortje to step in. Dortje gets the answer right and rolls a six, overtaking Sam. To Francesca's horror, Sam begins to cry. 'I'd have got it right the next time,' he sniffs. 'Why didn't you let me have another go?'

'You can't win all the time, Sam.' Francesca has ruined her cover and is speaking in broken German.

'Yes I can,' Sam wails.

'He always wins,' confirms Dani. 'We don't mind.'

'He cries like this if he doesn't,' adds Dortje.

'He needs a tissue,' says Dani, leaving the table to fetch one, 'it's not good when Sam cries and he's got a cold.'

'He snots a lot,' adds Thomas unnecessarily, illustrating the action with his movements.

ANJA IS READING a home-time story from a book that has been read so many times it's falling apart, breaking off to say goodbye as parents and guardians come to collect their children. Before Thomas leaves, he brings Francesca a piece of paper with a purple squiggle on it, explaining that it's a map of his house and Francesca is to come to eat that evening. 'What's for dinner?' Francesca asks smiling, but Thomas has already disappeared.

One by one, the rest of the children are summoned to change their shoes and get ready for the journey home. Sam clings to his father when he arrives. Dortje is reluctant to leave the carpet, where she is sitting next to Francesca. Dani wants to hear the end of the story, and is finally dragged away. Francesca smiles to herself when she hears the girl's father whisper the promise of an ice-cream. And soon there's only one child left, a little girl who listens obediently to the end of the story. The fairytale finishes with the heroine living happily ever after, and still there's no sign of anyone to collect Lily Richter.

'We'll wait another five minutes, and then I'll ask the office to phone,' whispers Anja while the girl is choosing a pop-up book to look at. 'It's unusual for Lily to be the last to be collected.'

Anja busies herself getting the classroom ready for the next day while Francesca sits with Lily as she flicks through the pages of *The Hungry Caterpillar*. 'Look, Lily, what's under here?' says Francesca, lifting a large green leaf.

'Lily!' A man stumbles into the room and Lily jumps into his arms. He hugs her tightly, as though drawing strength from her tiny body.

'Mr—' Anja begins, but the man waves her questions away. 'I'm sorry, I can't,' he mouths over Lily's head. 'I'll call the office tomorrow. Lily will be away for a little while, I'm afraid.'

'See you soon bye-bye,' chirps Lily over her father's shoulder as he carries her from the room. Francesca sees that he forgets to collect Lily's outdoor shoes that are hanging on a peg outside the classroom, but somehow she knows not to take them to him.

· · ·

AS THEY LEAVE THE BUILDING, Anja takes Francesca on a detour through the school's small gym. She stops in front of a large gold-framed photograph. At first, Francesca doesn't understand what Anja's showing her. She scans the picture but can't see anyone she recognises: just a sea of unknown children with dust on their clothes, and several matronly-looking women fading into the dark background like ghosts. Francesca glances at Anja for help.

'Look again!' Anja says, triumphant that she has been able to finish this pilgrimage for Francesca.

And then, third row down, squeezed in last on the right, Francesca finds a young girl who must be her mother squinting shyly at the camera. Standing taller besides her is Anja, looking glam and confident and holding on to her mother's arm as though they are friends.

11

'Mum, what happened to Anja and Richie's daughter?'

'Oh.' Imogen looks at her daughter in the mirror, where Francesca's applying some new make-up she'd bought on the way home with Anja. One eye is heavily made up, the other still bare of glittery eye shadow and gloopy black mascara. They are in the tiny green guest room – her parents' room. 'She told you?'

'I don't know if she meant to.'

'She was called Alexandra, for your father, I think. We were her godparents.'

Such a huge thing, Francesca thinks. Her parents had a goddaughter called Alexandra because of her father, and Francesca had known nothing about it at all. It's as though the girl had never existed.

'What happened to her?'

'Sometimes it's better not to talk about these things, Fran. She died when she was little. It's better not to delve.'

'Was she sick?' Francesca turns from the mirror to look directly at her mother.

'No, she wasn't,' Imogen says, sitting down on the bed. 'It was all such a long time ago.'

'That's so sad,' says Francesca, her heart thumping. 'But it's weird that there's no pictures or anything. If I died, you'd keep some photos of me up, right?'

'Nothing's going to happen to you, silly. And anyway, you don't like having your picture taken.'

'But if I did? You wouldn't just let everyone forget me?'

'We could never forget about you. And I don't think Anja's forgotten Alexandra. She mentioned her to you, didn't she? It's just a very difficult thing to live with.'

What is? Francesca wants to say, sensing her mother is on the brink of revelation, but still undecided as to whether to satisfy her daughter's curiosity.

'There you both are,' says Alex, forgetting to knock. 'I've had some ideas for Richie's birthday.'

'Hmm,' says Imogen. 'Yes, we can pick something up tomorrow.'

'But don't you want to know my ideas?'

Francesca exchanges a look with her father. They both know her mother *doesn't* want to hear his ideas – not now, anyway.

'*I* do, dad,' she says, to make up for it. She could see that for a second her father had been excited, and she hates her mother for taking that away from him. Anja had said that there would be lots of her parents' old friends at the party. It's in four days, and although everyone else is looking forward to it, her mother seems on edge whenever Richie's birthday or the party is mentioned. Francesca prays she isn't going to do anything embarrassing, or ruin Richie's birthday for him.

She thinks of the dress Anja had helped her pick out, a sliver of deep red waiting in Anja's wardrobe for the day of the party. She'd been meaning to show it to her mother as soon as she arrived home, but it doesn't feel right to now. She'll say something to steal the sheen from Francesca and Anja's joint purchase, and that'll be the beginning of her mother spoiling things for everyone.

Francesca's mind flicks back to the conversation her father had interrupted, to the revelations he may have aborted. She could ask her father she supposes, but somehow the name won't let her. It's just a word, a twist of fate, a vanity on Richie and Anja's behalf (and maybe her parents' too) but in those two letters the dead girl is forever linked to Francesca's dear, living father.

Francesca asks herself how she would frame the question for her father, how she would explain away the conversation she'd begun with her mother, but the connection is so strong that even as she holds the first word in her mouth with the sweet deliciousness of a secret about to be revealed, there's a revolt and Francesca finds herself coughing like there's a fly caught at the back of her tongue, right on the underside where she knows no-one will ever be able to reach it. She grasps to understand the connection, the link from her father to a dead child. Had the name simply been to honour a friendship? Or was it no more than a liking for the sharp sound of the word? *What is it* thinks Francesca, straining to understand, thinking that if she doesn't now, when she can still taste the twin words on her tongue, she never will. Her brain sparks against her father's name; then fizzles with a hiss. Everything stops, and she hasn't managed it.

She's aware of her parents talking, the cadence of their words suggestive of bickering even though her head hurts so much she can't concentrate, and something strange is swimming in her stomach. She leaves her parents and wanders through to the kitchen, where Anja is frying burgers for dinner, with shrivelled red onions that look like they hurt. *Water*, she thinks. *Water*.

Normally, Francesca loves burgers; her parents hardly ever have them at home, but this evening the smell and spit of the fat in the pan makes her retch before she can even reach the tap.

And then in an instant she remembers her smugness that she hadn't been sick on the flight out here, even though she'd witnessed that other girl throwing up in the aisle opposite, and smelt the rising stench of the girl's vomit as it had been trekked up and down the plane. *How embarrassing for her*, Francesca had thought, and the smell had intensified with each wave of the girl's imagined shame. When she'd realised the child had been travelling alone, Francesca's mother smiled at the girl, offering to help, but Francesca kept her nose pressed against the window, holding her breath until she thought her brain would burst.

It's the first time Francesca's thought about that day since they've arrived, and suddenly it hits her why everyone had been so jumpy, why the girl had been unable to keep the airline's food decently in her stomach. It hits her that she and her mother and everyone around them could easily have been caught up in the attack. That they could have died. She could have died on the way here, and she would never have known any of this: this foreign country, this suffocating flat, these people, this strange dead tale of the other Alex, this connection that scalds her whenever she goes to touch it.

She retches again, puking all the relief and fear and secrets into a puddle in the middle of Anja's kitchen floor.

12

———

Francesca wakes to the sound of buzzing. She slowly lifts her head and shakes it tentatively from side to side. She tries her legs, stretching them out so she can see her toes, with their chipped iridescent polish.

Anja and Richie's mattress is incredibly soft, so it's something of a struggle for her to climb out fully from under the huge duvet. Her body's sweating after spending a night buried under it, and she desperately needs the toilet.

Francesca identifies the buzzing as coming from her bag, which is on the floor by the bookcase, an orange light glowing through the snagged embroidery. She rummages through it and finds the small silver phone Antonio has given to her. She reads slowly: PARTY TONITE. MEET AT THE BAR AT 7.00. A.

It feels strange being in Richie and Anja's room. She remembers Anja and her mother putting her to bed, leaving her with a damp flannel on her forehead and a purple plastic bin besides the bed, which Francesca had vehemently protested she didn't need. Her mother said she should sleep in the spare room, not Anja and Richie's; that she and her father should be the ones taking the sofa for the night. After all, she'd implied, Francesca was her parents' problem, no-one else's. But Anja had insisted, and Francesca had sunk gratefully into a deliciously soft world, where she knew she would be able to sleep until the short circuit in her brain had repaired.

She looks around the room. There's a blurred photo of Anja and Richie kissing taped to the wall and an anniversary card from him to her on the ledge of the window. Francesca peers inside. The message is long, and Richie's writing is surprisingly feminine, with sweeping tails to his *f*s and *y*s. To Francesca, it seems a strange kind of place for a love letter – her parents' cards at anniversaries and birthdays and Valentines are always brief and to the point, barely varying with the year or occasion, signed with two kisses and left on public display in the living

room until they gather dust and her mother decides
the room is too cluttered. When Francesca was
twelve, she'd been horrified to discover that at the
point at which they begin collecting dust her mother
simply puts the cards out with the recycling – she
doesn't keep them safe, preserve them carefully in a
scrap-book, as Francesca would if they were hers.
Francesca concedes that perhaps at her mother's age
there is no longer a need for any trophies of love; but
she can't imagine there ever being a day where that
would be true of herself. If ever she were loved, she'd
keep every faded bus ticket; every cinema stub; every
scribbled postcard or hurried text.

And so Francesca burns as she reads Richie's de-
claration of love, its tone insistent and cajoling. She
can hardly separate the lines, but reads the whole of
it at once as though she's a machine taking a copy of
the page to pore over later.

*Du hast mich vor Jahren um Vergebung gebeten –
aber alles was ich tun kann ist dich zu lieben und darauf
warten das Du dir selbst vergibst.*

Richie's hand is shaking, the lines crammed in at
the bottom of the page. *Love* and *forgiveness*: she
knows those two words.

The prickles on her neck tell Francesca Anja is
in the room before Francesca can turn around. She
drops the card, her heart burnt black.

But it's nothing, no-one, and Francesca carefully

picks up the card and blows on it, as though she can erase her act of prying, before she sets it back on the window ledge, in almost exactly the same position it had stood before.

One of Richie's ties – an expensive kind of light blue – is hanging out of the chest of drawers. Francesca instinctively opens the drawer to put it back neatly for him. Ties, boxer shorts, pyjama bottoms and socks are all tangled up together. She closes the drawer quickly. Richie's a secret slob, like her.

Francesca walks over to the bookcase, and looks at the titles of the books. She can't understand most of them and wonders whether it's Richie or Anja who reads them. She decides on Anja. There's what looks like a photo album on the bottom shelf, but it's tightly wedged in and Francesca's worried Anja will think she's been snooping if she notices it's moved. Francesca aches to open it though – it looks old, private, and important, like one of her own memory books, and she thinks there might be something about Alexandra in it.

Alexandra. To think she'd never heard of her before yesterday. They would have been friends, she's sure. Francesca would have made her parents visit Berlin every year if she'd known Alexandra. And why's it such a secret what happened to her? *What-*

ever happened, happened in this flat, decides Francesca suddenly.

THAT EVENING, as Francesca approaches Antonio's bar she can see Antonio waiting outside, slouched against the window. Embarrassingly, she is accompanied by her father. It had been hard enough to persuade everyone she was well enough to go out, let alone that she could set off out into the city on her own. Her father would only let her out on the insistence that he came to meet Antonio himself. He couldn't see when Francesca had had time to make a friend in Berlin, and wasn't at all happy that she'd be out in the city at night on her own, especially after how ill she'd been yesterday. *One lie begets another*, Francesca had said to herself, thinking of *Macbeth* and wishing she'd tried telling her parents the truth about the morning she'd met Antonio. Or at least included him in the story. The trouble is that when Francesca's placed on the spot, with someone questioning her actions, she's not very good at making up stories. 'I met him on the internet, he's grooming me,' she had said, thinking she could stall with humour. Another girl would have got away with it, but when she'd said it the tone had been all wrong.

'Fantastic, Francesca. Your flippancy just confirms your irresponsible approach to life. You think we can trust you now?'

'Relax, dad. Antonio's my pen-pal. From school, remember?' She does have a pen-pal, it's true. 'We'd arranged to meet.'

'You don't even study German, Francesca.'

'It's not all about language, you know. It's about getting to know another culture, and its history. It's about tolerance too. School wants us to get to know someone from our generation from another country. So we understand each other better. I chose Germany, because of you. Charlotte's got someone from Norway. You know, we absolutely *have* to visit Checkpoint Charlie while we're here. You will take me, won't you, dad?'

Alex hadn't been sure whether to be touched by Francesca's choosing a German pen-pal and never telling him, or whether he needed to investigate why she was lying to him. You couldn't be too careful. Only this morning he'd read about a teenage girl who'd been cyber-bullied by a neighbour – a 38-year-old woman pretending to be a teenage boy. The girl had thought she was having a relationship with the boy, and when the messages had turned nasty, she'd hung herself. So Alex decided the only responsible thing to do was to meet Antonio for himself. Only then could he judge the boy's intentions. Francesca had drawn the line at the whole family coming, although Richie had looked almost a little sad at being left at home.

WHEN ANTONIO SEES Francesca and her father he straightens, takes his cap off and steps forward. Francesca squirms, hoping Antonio has seen her text message.

But then, even if Antonio has seen the text, Francesca's not sure he would have understood it.

HAD TO TELL DAD U WERE PENPAL. WE'VE NEVER MET, BUT KNOW EACH OTHER FROM LETTERS ORGANISED BY SCHOOL. U HAVE TO SAY U STILL GO TO SCHOOL. OK?

FOR THE LAST HOUR, Francesca has been frantically hoping that Antonio is able to act suitably formal and penpal-ish. She's even considered not going to meet him anymore, and had told her dad she thought she was getting a headache (she was, from all the panicking), but that had only seemed to rouse his suspicion further.

As they approach the meeting point, the moment when her lie will either be given life or de-stroyed and exposed, Francesca feels like she's going to faint.

Antonio steps forward, his cap in his hands. He looks awfully tall for a schoolboy. 'Pleased to meet you,' he says in perfect English, shaking hands with Alex.

'Pleased to meet you, I'm Francesca's father,' says Alex, before switching to German and speaking too fast for Francesca to catch his meaning.

Antonio looks confused. 'I'm an apprentice mechanic. I'm at college two days a week,' he replies in English.

Gotcha thinks Alex, turning to his daughter.

'We started being pen-pals when you were still at school, didn't we Antonio?'

'Yes,' says Antonio, grinning and putting his cap back on. 'Nice to meet you, Francesca. You look like your photo.' He looks at his watch. 'Would you like to come to the party too, sir? It's my sister Ingrid's birthday. My family would be very pleased to meet you.'

Francesca finally lets herself relax as her father gruffly declines. It's enough for him to have the phone number and address of the party, although Francesca notices a slight frown as he works out the location of the block of flats. He's heard unsavoury things about this area, and Alex is caught between his liberal upbringing and a sharp concern for his only daughter's safety. He wishes he hadn't been so gung-ho about bringing Francesca out here on his own, but to have to confer with his wife at this stage is unthinkable, and so with a quick peck on the fore-head, he lets Francesca go.

'WHY DID YOU LIE?' asks Antonio on the tram. Francesca shrugs. 'It just seemed easier,' she says, starting to laugh. 'I thought for a minute he really would come with us.'

'It would have been okay. My family would have welcomed him. It would have been fun.'

'It would not have been fun,' counters Francesca. 'Anyway, I need a break from them.'

Antonio just smiles. The tram's busy and Francesca's head is almost on his shoulder. He can smell her shampoo. English apples, he thinks. Bramley, Cox. He'd once answered an exam paper on English apples.

FRANCESCA HAS NEVER FELT as welcomed anywhere as she does the moment the door opens in the tiny high-rise flat Antonio shares with his mum and sister. Everyone is interested in *die Engländerin*, as Antonio calls her. She meets Antonio's uncle Gus who owns *Die Lustige Riesen*; his sister Ingrid, she's tall like Antonio; his little cousins Hanna and Hugo who spend the whole evening eating chocolate cake. Neither their mother nor Antonio's mother Maria seem to mind them eating so much – every so often one of them good-naturedly wipes the chocolate from the children's mouths. Francesca eventually gives up trying to keep the children's messy hands and faces at arm's length. After a while, she doesn't bother even trying to brush the dried chocolate from her jeans. With Hanna on her lap and Hugo crawling at her feet, Francesca accepts a third slice of cake. It seems that as long as her family and loved ones are fed and happy, Maria is content.

Ingrid is also very happy to meet Francesca. She wants to practise her English; she's doing a business qualification and hopes to work in London when it's finished. Her English is much better than Antonio's.

'I actually studied when I was at school. Antonio just turned up. He was in the building but his mind was on other things,' Ingrid explains, speaking purposely fast. 'The school hero,' she adds, and Francesca struggles to interpret her sarcasm.

Antonio looks hurt. 'You say my English iz not good?'

His mother hurries to reassure him. 'Both my children are *perfekt*,' she says, giving each of them a kiss. 'They'd do anything for their mama. I'm very lucky. I don't know what I'd do without them.'

'Shush, mama,' says Ingrid. 'Mum always starts this when I talk about going to live in London,' she explains quietly to Francesca. 'My aunt and uncle and the rest of our family only live up the street, but she still says doesn't want to be left all alone when we leave.'

'Who's leaving?' interrupts Maria. 'I won't have talk of leaving. I don't know what I'd do without my children near me. You have good home. Nice bed. Loving Mama. Why anyone want to leave?'

ON THE WAY back to Anja and Richie's, Francesca asks Antonio about his father. He appears surprised to be asked, as if he's not talked about his father for many years.

'He left when I was five; he has another family now. They live near München. Big house, nice car.'

Francesca thinks of the flat she's just left. Antonio and Ingrid each have a room, but when she'd asked where the third bedroom was, she'd been shocked to learn that Antonio's mother sleeps every night in the living room.

'I know I should move out,' Antonio had explained. 'But she won't hear of it. And she won't let me and Ingrid share like we did when we were little; she thinks that would drive one of us out.' Something would have to change soon, he'd said, but he couldn't imagine what stunt his mother might pull to keep them both at home.

'Do you visit him?' Francesca asks, although she suspects she already knows the answer.

'Once. When I was seven. He used to send me a cheque for a hundred Euro every birthday and Christmas. I stopped putting them in the bank when I was ten. He stopped sending them when I was twelve. I could be a rich man!'

They walk on in silence, and Antonio slips Francesca's hand into his. It feels nice, warm, and for a moment the whole world stops. She can feel the nerve ends tingling in her fingers, as though every touch can zap a message right through to Antonio.

A thousand tiny shocks pass between them.

THEY COME to some traffic lights, and Antonio introduces Francesca to the Ampelmann – East Berlin's special traffic-light man.

'See, he's friendly. He wears a hat. He tells you when to cross!'

The road's busy and Francesca sees a young woman on the opposite pavement, swaying dangerously close to the flow of traffic. She instinctively takes a step back. A man opens his car window and shouts at the woman to get out of the way. The girl gestures rudely in response, staggers forward and collapses in the road.

Antonio pulls Francesca after him across the road, dodging the traffic. Francesca's squeal of dissent is drowned by the wail of a gigantic red lorry sounding its horn at them.

13

'It's okay, Lena. Let me help you up. Let's get you sorted.' Antonio pulls the young woman to her feet; gently easing open the girl's shaking fist and placing it on his shoulder for support. She pushes Antonio away, reminding Francesca of a sulky child. Antonio holds on to her as a car speeds past, giving a long low beep. 'Francesca, meet Lena. Lena, meet Francesca.'

Francesca looks at her watch. She has half an hour to get back for her curfew.

'Hurry, Antonio. We need to get her out of the road.'

Three red cars flash past, and they all seem to be saying the same thing Francesca's thinking.

The girl glares, though her eyes fill with tears.

'An early breakfast, that'll sober her up.'

'Will anywhere be open?' Francesca asks anxiously. A young couple cross the road, looking at the three of them curiously as they pass.

'Y' want food? I know a place,' says Lena, swaying close against Antonio like they're dancing. 'S'just around the corner.'

'On we go then. Lead the way,' says Antonio, bearing Lena's weight.

'Antonio, can I talk to you a minute?' Francesca asks.

'Sure,' says Antonio, waiting for her to speak. Francesca can see he can't let go of Lena without having to go through the whole rigmarole of picking her up again. So she has to talk about Lena as though she's not there.

'Can't we just move her away from the road? Or can't you call someone to help? We need to hurry if I'm not going to be late.'

'Of course you can leave. Don't trouble yourself for me.' To Francesca's horror, Lena starts to cry again. This time it's louder, a wail that merges with the sound of the passing cars.

'She's just drunk.'

'She needs our help. We'll get her to the café, then I'll take you home. There's plenty of time. We can't leave her here.'

Everyone else would, Francesca wants to protest. *I would.*

She tries again, palms sweating. 'Listen Antonio, I'm going to be in real trouble if I don't get back on time. We agreed with my dad, remember?'

The cars remember. They all know. As a battered blue Volkswagen screeches to a stop at the traffic lights she thinks she hears a last warning to run home while she can.

AT THE CAFÉ, Lena slides into a booth, leaning her head against the window. She lights a cigarette and gives a long hacking cough, her head bumping against the glass. Antonio slides in opposite and orders a coffee and a bacon sandwich for Lena. He asks to pay right away, leaving the waitress a good tip.

'You're not leaving her here, are you?' the young waitress asks, timidly. 'I'm on my own, and I have to close up in an hour.'

'I'll have a glass of milk,' says Antonio, apparently skimming the menu for whatever's cheapest. 'And one slice of toast.'

Francesca sighs, for the moment resigning herself to being late. There's not much else she can do. 'Do you have any ice-cream?' she asks.

'Of course,' says the waitress.

· · ·

'YOU WANT TO KNOW ABOUT TONIGHT?' Lena asks, wiping ketchup from her mouth.

'Sure,' says Antonio while Francesca sits with her head on the table, pretending to sleep. She's finished her banana split, and is waiting for Antonio to finish his milk. He's taking forever, swilling it around in the glass, drinking in tiny sips. Lena, Francesca's realised, is in the mood to talk, and the more she talks the angrier Francesca feels at Antonio, who doesn't seem to be doing anything to curb Lena's emotions or bring the situation to a resolution. He simply sits and listens, as though he has enough time to give some to Lena as a gift.

'You know how it feels, right? To think you finally have a home, and then everything changes.' Her eyes challenge Francesca's, and though Francesca can now see there are just a few years between them, Francesca doesn't know. 'The old bitch has really done it this time. She's thrown me out.'

Antonio explains that Lena lives with her grandmother and Lena fills in the never-ending arguments about Lena's boyfriend, Jay.

'Perhaps he'll pick you up?' Francesca suggests hopefully, deciding she'll have to be the one to sort things out.

FRANCESCA CAN'T BELIEVE Antonio's plan. Not only

has he offered to let Lena sleep in his uncle's bar, but all three of them are now on the way to Lena's grandmother's house to collect some of her things. Francesca feels sick. She's already extremely late; she doesn't know how to get home; she hasn't programmed her dad's number into the phone she's borrowing, despite his telling her to; and Antonio is insisting on the detour to the grandmother's house. Life couldn't get any worse.

'I'll explain everything to your parents. We've got to help Lena, don't we?' Antonio keeps saying like a big dumb Labrador puppy.

'If Lena's story is true, how's taking her back there going to help?'

'I need my stuff,' wheedles Lena.

'Can't you buy a toothbrush?'

'Antonio's going to help me get my stuff,' insists Lena.

'Well, I'm not coming in,' says Francesca. 'This is a big mistake.'

'Shhh,' says Lena, 'this is the street. This is where I live.'

Francesca looks down the narrow road. She doesn't know why Lena's trying to get her to be quiet – she can hear a couple arguing through one of the windows, and there's obviously a party going on in one of the houses.

The communal bins are overflowing and among

the domestic debris, there's an abandoned mattress lying across the pavement.

'Been here for weeks,' says Lena, as they pick their way across the spongy surface, which Francesca thinks must be like walking on the moon.

Lena stops outside a small house with a broken wooden gate. It creaks as she opens it. She arches an eyebrow at Francesca. 'You're waiting here?' Francesca looks at the house opposite, where a television is lighting up one of the rooms like strobes at a disco. A burst of raucous laughter is accompanied by the sound of a slamming door. Francesca shakes her head, and follows Lena into the house, holding on to Antonio's jacket.

'WE'RE DECORATING,' Lena explains, as the smell of drying paint hits Francesca's nose. At the bottom of the stairs, Francesca glimpses the kitchen, stacked high with dirty dishes. As she climbs the steep narrow stairway, she feels something soft brush against her legs and almost screams. Lena turns at the sharp intake of breath. 'Shhh,' she hisses bossily.

After that, Francesca's heart refuses to slow down. What's she doing here, she thinks. It's crazy that she's managed to get caught up in this strange girl's life. Of course, it's all Antonio's fault –

Francesca doesn't normally even speak to strangers. She broke that by bursting into Antonio's bar, and now look what's happened. Across the landing, Francesca can see a large grey cat staring at her, its white-tipped tail moving lazily from side to side. Francesca desperately wants to break the silence. 'I shouldn't be here,' she wants to shout over and over, until somebody hears. 'I'm supposed to be at home.'

LENA PUSHES the door in front of her open. It sticks against the too thick carpet. *Oh no*, thinks Francesca, *it's the old lady's bedroom.* Antonio follows Lena into the room without glancing back at her. Francesca wonders whether to stay on the landing with the malevolent cat or whether to stick with Antonio. She wipes her palms on her jeans as though she's about to shake someone's hand.

Inside the room, a woman sits by the window, her back to the three of them as though refusing them entry. The air is stale and the room lit by a single bedside lamp with a dying bulb. Francesca stares at the bobbly carpet. It's Antonio who speaks first, and Francesca thinks how much of the language she has absorbed, for she understands the sense of the German even where the precise word or phrase is unknown to her. Anja is right, of course. *Nothing teaches better than necessity.*

'We bought Lena to collect some things. We're not here to disturb you.'

The woman turns to look at Antonio like she doesn't understand. 'Not the boyfriend, then,' she says. 'He'll be out causing trouble. Why aren't you with him, Lena? I should never have—'

'Go ahead, Lena. Get your things.'

Francesca sees that Lena's crying. She's not letting the sound out – she doesn't want them to know. Now she wants to drag Lena away, to drag them all from this terrible room with its stale air and secrets.

The old woman looks right into Francesca's eyes, as though seeing her there on the carpet for the first time. 'Get out. We don't need you here. Get out of our home,' she says slowly, her voice hoarse. 'Go. Get the fuck out of here.'

Francesca flees, not waiting to see what Antonio is going to do. She stumbles down the stairs in the dark, disturbing one of the cats. It hisses at her and follows her to the door, where she fumbles with the latch. It won't open. Her hands won't stop shaking and the door won't open. She's trapped here forever, and her parents will never know where she is or what happened to her. They'll make up stories about her at school, and no one will ever know the truth about what happened to Francesca Maier in Berlin.

At the touch of Antonio's hand on her back, Francesca screams, shrill and high.

'Shhhh, calm down Fran,' Antonio whispers, firmly pushing her hands away and opening the door himself. Francesca breaks into a run, past the abandoned mattress and overflowing bins, not waiting to check which way she should turn at the end of the street.

14

As they near Anja and Richie's neighbourhood, Francesca waits for Antonio to apologise. He doesn't. He's thinking about Lena.

'Did we do the right thing leaving her there?' he asks.

Francesca glares at him in exasperation. 'I'm going to be grounded for a really long time,' she says.

'Maybe I'll check up on her tomorrow.'

'You're crazy, Antonio. You can't just keep letting yourself get caught up in other people's problems.'

'That's what my mum says, English girl. But then I wouldn't have met you, would I?' says Antonio, suddenly playful again. 'Anyway, your father likes me, I can tell.'

'I don't think so, Antonio. And you do know we only made things worse? You thought we had to stop and help, but we didn't help, did we? We made things a whole lot worse!' Francesca shakes her head to try to dislodge the memory of the old woman's angry words. They stick in her ears like water after she's been swimming.

'You'd better come in,' says Francesca's father to Antonio, not taking his eyes off Francesca for a second. 'We were close to calling the police. I phoned your mother; she said you'd left the party hours ago. What have you been doing with my daughter until now?'

Her mother appears. 'Really Francesca, we're all very disappointed. Every time we give you a little freedom, a little responsibility—'

One of Anja and Richie's neighbours, a teenage boy a little older than Francesca, squeezes past her father in the doorway. He's on his way out, and several bottles of what looks like beer clink in his shopping bag. 'Have you any idea what we've been thinking? And to do this in Anja and Richie's house, to make us have to behave like—'

'It's disrespectful, Francesca.' Francesca knows that once they get into the full flow of telling her off, her parents make an excellent tag team, interchangeably finishing one another's points, picking up the slack where one's lost track of the argument. It's so unfair, she thinks, like playing tennis two against one.

Richie appears in the doorway.

'Perhaps we should discuss this inside,' he suggests timidly, perhaps thinking of the neighbours, perhaps hoping Imogen's not going to turn on him after the telling off she gave him at the beach. Richie notices Antonio, and steps forward to introduce himself, formality taking over.

'Don't let him get away,' says Alex through gritted teeth, prepared to physically restrain Antonio. 'Apparently, he's Francesca's pen-pal.'

'About that, dad...'

'No need, Francesca. I've spoken to Charlotte's mother, and Charlotte didn't know anything about any pen-pals – Norwegian, German, or otherwise.' He turns to Antonio. 'So what I want to know is this: who the hell are you, and how do you know my daughter?'

UPSTAIRS, Antonio sits wedged awkwardly between Francesca's parents on the sofa. He's taken his cap off and holds it in his hands, running his fingers over the logo. Anja is making everyone a hot chocolate, while Alex paces the room preparing to begin the interrogation and Francesca hovers nervously, wondering if she's about to be sent to bed, or murdered.

'You're right dad, Antonio's not my pen-pal,' Francesca offers. 'I just said that.'

'Oh?'

'I didn't know how to explain. Antonio saved me, you see.'

'He saved you?' Anja asks, walking in with a tray of drinks, complete with biscuits on a china plate. 'That sounds intriguing.'

'Yes, do go on Fran,' says her mother, speaking with a dangerous calmness.

'I got lost, you see. There was this man, at the tram stop. He wanted to talk to me, and when I didn't want to talk back he started chasing me. And then I dropped the money I'd got with me, and I was lost, and I had nothing with me to help me get back, and Antonio saved me. He scared away the man who was following me, closed the bar and brought me home. So we're friends.'

'There's a bar?' asks Alex. 'You were in a bar?'

'I didn't know it was a bar. It was just somewhere with people in it, somewhere safe. Nothing else was open. I didn't know where I was.'

'You know you're not old enough to go in bars, Fran.'

'I think you're missing the point, Imogen. Francesca was in trouble,' says Richie.

Francesca's mother shoots Richie a look that says *you know nothing about bringing up teenagers.*

'And I think Francesca's missing a very big point,' says Alex. 'Which is, what were you doing at the tram stop anyway? When was this, and who gave you permission?'

Because Antonio's there, and Richie and Anja too, Francesca resists the urge to shout the hate that's building in her bones and run from the room. She's also determined not to cry.

'It was the day we left the lake-house. You wouldn't wake up, and I was bored. I just wanted to explore.'

'Ah, so you lied?' Alex says. 'There's no excuse for lying, Fran. Especially not being bored. After all, we can't be there to entertain you all the time, can we?' He looks across at Imogen, seeking reassurance that it wasn't their fault Francesca had been so thoughtless.

'You lied to us,' Imogen reiterates.

'Well, I think we're lucky Francesca ran into Antonio. Who knows what would have happened if Antonio hadn't been there, and the horrible man who'd been following Fran had caught her up?' Anja shivers. 'I think Antonio's a hero,' she adds, smiling at him warmly.

'We haven't even started talking about tonight yet,' says Alex. 'Perhaps you shouldn't be in such a hurry to award the boy a knighthood.'

'Where's this bar you work in, Antonio? I might know it...' Anja smiles encouragingly at Antonio, letting him know she's on his side – nothing bad's going to happen to him in *her* house.

OUTSIDE, Francesca gets a few snatched minutes alone with Antonio.

'Sorry for all that,' she whispers. 'You know, you didn't have to stay for so long.'

Antonio just smiles. 'It was nothing,' he says, removing his cap and putting it back on at a minutely different angle. 'Sorry I got you home late.' He touches her nose lightly, and her stomach flips over.

'At least Anja likes you,' Francesca says quickly, pleased at the apology. 'I can't believe she invited you to dinner.'

15

After everyone's finally gone to bed, Francesca presses her nose against the tank and whispers to the fish. It seems strange to share a room with other living beings and not attempt to communicate with them. She likes the plain goldfish best. He looks like he's listening. 'What do you make of that, Goldie?' she asks the fish, having detailed the hand-holding incident. It's the one memory she's salvaged from the day, before the strange encounter with Lena and her anger at Antonio's logic. She can close her eyes and be back in the moment. It's not like she's in love or anything, it's just nice that Antonio had wanted to hold her hand. Although now she thinks about it, she's not sure who had reached for whose hand first. Had her hand strayed too close to his, making Antonio think she wanted to hold his hand before he'd thought of it himself? She'd attributed the action to him, but when she tries to think of exactly what happened before they were holding hands, she can't.

And, weirdly, Anja had helped Francesca get out of trouble with her parents again. It seems disloyal to talk about this with Goldie, but Francesca wonders why she still can't feel at ease with Anja. Anja just seems to be trying to help, like she doesn't see why Francesca should be in trouble so much, and yet Francesca can't help feeling suspicious of her. When Anja had invited Antonio to dinner, she'd made it sound as though she simply wanted to repay Antonio for his family's hospitality, and for looking out for Francesca when she'd been lost. That made sense. It was a nice thing to do. And yet Francesca doesn't know why, but she really doesn't want the evening to take place. Part of her feels that Antonio is the only friend she has here, and somehow she wants to protect that.

And then of course, there's the mystery of Alexandra. Francesca's determined to get to the bottom of what happened to the little girl, to unearth the secret. It's almost like we're twins, she thinks. Alexandra's my ghost-twin. She repeats the word as she tries to get comfortable on the lumpy sofa-bed mattress. *Ghost-twin, ghost-twin, what would it be like if you were really here?*

Thinking about Alexandra, for some reason Francesca remembers overhearing her mother and Anja in the lake-house that first morning. There seems to have been something simmering between them ever since. What is it? A mutual dislike? That doesn't seem right – there are moments when Francesca thinks she can see all the way through to the old friendship between them, that there is a deep connection between the two women. But something always holds them back from each other. What was it Anja had said? 'Then it was worth it.' Her mother had done something in the past, made some kind of sacrifice. If only Francesca could just ask her mother what all the strange behaviour was about. But of course her mother would tell her she was imagining things. And her father's more interested in catching Francesca out. Somehow, though, Francesca thinks there's more to worry about than any trouble she might get into.

AT BREAKFAST THE NEXT DAY, her father is brooding and silent. It's a dangerous mood for him to be in; if they were at home, Francesca would disappear to her room until it had passed. Her mother looks like she's got a headache. Only Richie attempts conversation, trying to make everyone laugh with goofy jokes Francesca doesn't understand. Today she thinks she hates being in a foreign country – she's not sure whether it's her funny bone that's been stolen or Richie's. Anja's already left for work, and Francesca guesses the sightseeing plans for the day have been cancelled. Although it's sticky-warm and sunny outside, inside it's like it's a rainy day and Francesca's caused it.

She tries showing she's sorry by talking about Germany, showing her dad how much she's listened to him while they've been here, showing how interested she is in his culture, his roots. She loves the houses, she says, they're all so different. She loves the lakes, the people, the districts, the tramlines, the snack stands, the language, everything. Her father lets Francesca chatter on, angry and unimpressed.

'I feel like I'm learning so much here, you know?' Francesca finishes hopefully. 'I wish we'd come here every summer – I'd be fluent by now. In fact, we should get a house here. You should design it, dad. What do you think?' Her father smiles dryly. Francesca cracks. 'Look dad, I'm really sorry, okay? I didn't want to be late. I wanted to be at home. I was so stressed about being late – you should have heard me. "My parents are going to kill me," I kept saying. But I couldn't get back without Antonio, and he was helping Lena, who would probably be dead by now, or sleeping on the streets, if we hadn't been looking after her. So in a way I was just being a good citizen, like we're taught in citizenship classes, like the Good Samaritan. And I'm sorry I lied to you about Antonio being a pen-pal. That was stupid. He's just someone I met, and I didn't think you'd understand.'

'It's okay, Fran. We know you didn't mean to cause so much trouble. We were just worried about you,' her mother says, eager to draw a line under the scene, as though suddenly aware that they are not in the privacy of their own home. As though, some-how, with Richie here, she feels they are under scru-tiny – that whatever is said will be passed back to Anja. She leans across the table to pat Francesca's hair into place. 'No-one's cross with you anymore. It's okay.' But Francesca looks across at her father and knows that it isn't.

FRANCESCA SPENDS the rest of the day keeping as much of out everyone's way as she can, doing penance. She pretends to read one of Anja's books in the corner, translating with the help of a large German–English dictionary, but really she's day-dreaming. She starts out re-living holding hands with Antonio, progressing to imagining their first proper kiss, by the lake she thinks, and to her hor-ror, she finds herself thinking of Richie. It isn't the first time she's thought of Richie like this. Ever since she's arrived he's intruded on her thoughts at weird times, but since the lost promise of the new phone she's been at pains to avoid thinking of him as anything other than her father's friend. It doesn't help that he's so charming. Much more charming than Antonio, who seems awkward and out of place anywhere but his uncle's bar. Antonio hadn't even really bothered to flirt with her; he'd just taken her hand and bypassed all that. Whereas Richie, she thinks, Richie flirts when he breathes.

'Are you okay, Fran?' Richie asks.

Oh Jesus, he can read my thoughts, Francesca thinks, panicking.

'You sighed.'

'Yeah, it's just my book.' What did she say that for? What will he think she's reading?

'You need some help with the translation?'

Actually, there are a few words Francesca had been stuck on before she started daydreaming, but she suspects from the context they could be dangerous ones to ask for a public translation of. She shakes her head, and Richie grins.

'Well, let me know.'

WHEN ANJA ARRIVES home in the afternoon, Francesca is glad the pressure-cooker atmosphere is finally relieved. Anja is hardly through the door when Francesca offers to help with the evening's meal.

'Of course. It's something special, in honour of our guest.'

'Do you need me to go to the shops with you?' Francesca asks hopefully. She hasn't been out all day, and there isn't even a proper window to open anywhere in the flat. They're all blocked up in some way, or painted shut.

'I got everything on the way home. Wash your hands and you can start chopping the vegetables.'

Francesca starts with the carrots and the onions, while Anja chooses some music for them to cook to. Alex wanders into the kitchen and out again. Anja winks at Francesca, as if to say 'watch this'.

'Is everything alright, Alex? Are you hungry?'

Alex hovers in the doorway. 'Are you cooking for this boy too?'

'For Antonio, yes.'

'You've invited this boy to dinner?'

'Antonio, yes.'

'Hmmph.' Alex walks into the kitchen, inspects the chopped onions, picking some up as though to say they're the wrong size, turns on his heel and leaves.

'He'll be good as gold, you watch,' says Anja conspiratorially. 'Your father couldn't be impolite if he tried.' Francesca's borrowed phone buzzes. 'Is that

Antonio? Tell him not to be late,' says Anja, glancing at the flashing screen before Francesca picks the phone up to read its message.

HELD UP ON WAY. MITE BE LATE, SORRY. A

Francesca starts to compose a reply instructing Antonio that in no way can he be late, but deletes the message halfway through, realising the impossibility of fighting whatever force has railroaded his plans. If Antonio thinks he needs to be late, he'll be late.

'YOU DIDN'T TELL them I'd be late?' Antonio asks, seeing everyone but Francesca and Anja seated around the table picking at oven-warm bread rolls, and Francesca's father glowering across the room at him.

Before Francesca can think what to say, Anja kisses Antonio on both cheeks and tells him not to worry. 'I'm sure you had your reasons,' she says, removing her blue-striped apron and smoothing down her long charcoal-grey dress. 'Sit, eat,' she says, gesturing to his place next to Francesca's.

Antonio removes his cap, smiles round at everyone and helps himself to some bread before taking his chair. 'Nice fish,' he says, gesturing at Emilio, whose mottled face is pressed up against the glass as though he's eavesdropping. Richie tells Antonio that he buys all his fish from a man who lives at Tempelhof airport, and Imogen explains about the news segment on animal behaviour they'd been talking about introducing at work. Antonio is hugely impressed to hear that Francesca's mother works in television.

'You're the presenter? I can't believe I'm talking to a news presenter! It's like eating with royalty or something!'

Francesca tries to explain, 'No, she's not on the television; she decides what goes on the television. Like researching, or editing, or writing what the presenters are going to say.'

Antonio looks deflated. 'You've never been on television?'

'Once. But not so as anybody would see.'

'That's cool, though.'

'Yeah, it is, isn't it?' says Francesca, smiling at her mum. Her mum's job always impresses people.

'Tell us about yourself, Antonio,' says Anja, nodding encouragingly once she has served goulash to everyone.

Francesca listens nervously as Antonio explains that he lives with his mum and sister in East Berlin and works as a trainee mechanic, adding that as part of his course at college he has to learn English and that he has a *very* important final exam coming up.

Alex sniffs and struggles with his stew, spilling some on his pale green shirt. 'You should try getting yourself a pen-pal.'

'Yes, I want to. I hope to keep in touch. But I think you mean Francesca's story?'

Francesca flushes. 'Dad—'

'Come on Alex, the girl made something up. You can't punish her forever. Enjoy your food.' Anja speaks briskly, as though challenging Alex to disobey her. Francesca sends a quick prayer of thanks in Anja's direction. Despite being a declared atheist, Francesca and her friends have always held that sometimes everyone needs to pray.

Alex inhales, about to launch an attack, checked by the table's need for propriety. 'Would you pass the bread, Fran?'

UNDER THE TABLE, Antonio's hand brushes Francesca's. To her relief, everyone appears to be getting on. Anja is filling her mother in on people they used to know. There's a strange story about two of their friends who'd married shortly after Francesca's mother and father had left Berlin, had two children each, and then, six years later, swapped husbands. They'd mixed up the children too, so each new family was made up of one of the wife's children, and one of her new husband's.

'You don't believe me?' Anja asks. 'We can meet up with Eleanor next week if you like. She'll probably invite us to her place. She couldn't have known at the time but it's been a lucrative swap for her.'

'And Sylvia?' Imogen asks.

'They moved away, to Vienna last time I heard. I've lost touch, and it doesn't seem right to ask Eleanor. I think she wanted to drop off the radar for a while, if you know what I mean. Most people come back, though. Eventually. If the people who stay in the same place wait around long enough. We all end up circling one another before too long, don't we!'

'It must be terrible for the children.'

'Maybe. Maybe not,' says Richie, finishing his dessert and rejoining the conversation. 'Who knows that one experience is better than another?'

'Watch out – Mr Philosophy's here to play,' says Anja, getting up to clear the table. 'You know Imogen, I'm actually pretty glad Richie never finished his degree. I only have to live with occasional bouts of philosophizing.'

'What do you think, Antonio?' Alex asks, while Anja's in the kitchen.

'I think Richie's right. How can we know what's best?'

'Ah, so you think there's no difference between right and wrong?'

'I think the easiest view isn't always the right one,' says Antonio with a shrug.

Alex takes a moment to consider Antonio's response.

'Daddy—' begins Francesca nervously, knowing her father is choosing between a long list of complaints, all revolving around Antonio's behaviour concerning herself.

'Touché,' says Alex, reaching across to shake Antonio's hand. 'Tell me more about this apprenticeship of yours.'

To Francesca's amazement, her father seems to be offering Antonio a truce. But will it last, she wonders, remembering the numerous false truces she's been involved in with her parents herself. Her father could very well just be loosening his grip, so as to persuade Antonio he is no longer a threat before launching his most brutal attack.

'I wonder how Lena is?' Francesca asks idly, while her father's talking to Richie.

'Okay, I think,' says Antonio. 'I'm seeing her tomorrow.'

'Good,' says Francesca, suddenly feeling as though the three of them are old friends. 'I'll come.'

16

When Francesca returns carrying hot drinks for everyone, the mood seems to have lightened. The three men are deep in conversation, and her mother is curled up on the sofa looking more relaxed than Francesca's seen her since the two of them had set off for the airport over a week ago. Antonio says something about having to leave soon, and Francesca's amazed to hear her father protest.

'You haven't told us that story about your uncle's trip to Poland yet.'

'Well, he didn't know the police had been following him from before the border. Broken taillight. He thought they wanted him for smuggling cheap jumpers and lighter fluid. He phoned me from

Poland, asking if he should abandon the car. Terrible mess, he was.'

'And what did you tell him?'

'I told him he'd have to find somewhere to lie low for a while. Preferably a forest. He believed me. Got so scared I had to drive out and fetch him.'

'Reminds me of Imogen's father,' says Alex, laughing. 'He always thinks someone's out to get him. I could make up the most outrageous conspiracy theory and he'd believe me. He'll hear the silliest thing and ponder on it for months. Thinks he communed with the dead when he was a teenager playing with a Ouija board.'

'Well, it's better than being a sceptic all your life, Alex,' says Imogen.

'I agree,' says Anja. 'Who knows what's out there?'

'Don't tell me you of all people believe in the afterlife, Anja? I wouldn't have thought—'

Francesca watches as her mother instinctively covers one of Anja's hands with her own, and her father lets his sentence hang unfinished, realising his mistake.

'I don't think you can know what you'll believe until you've lost someone,' Anja says quietly.

'Of course not,' says Alex. 'I'm sorry. I was insensitive. I didn't mean anything by it.'

'After we lost Alexandra, I would have done any-thing to be able to talk to my daughter again. But I was also terrified of the possibility. I couldn't watch any of those films that dealt with it, you know. The dead not dying.'

'I spoke without thinking. I'm sorry to bring it back, Anja.'

'Just because we don't talk about it doesn't mean it ever went anywhere, Alex. It still happened. My daughter still existed.'

'Of course. I'm being clumsy.' Alex looks over at his wife, as though hoping she'll help him out. 'I can't imagine what you both went through. We wor-ried about you. We might not have been here, but we did worry.'

'I know. You sent a card.'

'We wanted to do more. We should have done more. We should have been at the funeral.' Again, he looks at Imogen, who is keeping resolutely quiet.

Anja starts to laugh. 'Is that what you've been thinking about all these years? Trust me Alex, you don't need to worry about that. About whether you turned up at the funeral. Now that's funny. That's the last thing you have to worry about. The funeral.' And suddenly the laughter has turned to tears and Anja is sobbing. At least, Francesca thinks she's crying – there seems to be some kind of a struggle going on, which for once Anja is losing, resulting in a series of strange strangled noises.

Francesca glances at Richie. He looks bewildered, lost. *Go to her*, Francesca thinks, but he doesn't. Instead, it's Antonio who looks directly at Anja and asks if there's anything she needs – a drink, a walk. He has to leave soon anyway, so it seems a natural solution for them to get some air together, and everyone else seems relieved that Antonio is here, and prepared to shoulder the burden of comforting Anja.

'If you're sure,' says Richie to Antonio at the door, as though the only thing to worry about is whether Antonio's happy about having Anja foisted on him.

'It's been good to see you, Antonio. Who knows, we might check that bar of yours out in the next few days. Leave the women behind though, eh, Rich?' There's an uncomfortable silence as everyone takes in the idea that *the women* are too emotional for a decent night out. 'I didn't mean—' begins Alex, holding up his hands.

'You coming, Fran?' Antonio asks after he's hugged everyone goodbye.

'No, I'm not,' says Francesca, making a sudden decision. 'I'll see you tomorrow, though.'

And then Antonio and Anja are gone and the

house suddenly feels empty. Richie fetches Alex another beer from the kitchen. Imogen flicks rapidly though one of Anja's magazines, as though daring Francesca to ask her something.

'I THINK we can afford to let Fran have a little more freedom. After all – it's her holiday too.' Alex speaks to the breakfast table as though it's a collective decision, but everyone knows he'd been unexpectedly charmed by Antonio the previous evening. When he'd asked Imogen what she thought about the situation just as she was falling asleep, she'd murmured that he was just a boy after all. Maybe it wouldn't be such a bad idea to give him a chance, to get to know him a little. And after all, thought Alex after his wife was sleeping; it wasn't his place to stop his daughter making friends.

'As long as you're sensible, Fran. And keep in touch.'

'And stick to the plans we arrange, and don't make up any more stories.' Her parents are back to being an exemplary tag-team, Francesca notices, wondering why they hadn't been able to deploy the same skills in speaking to Anja the night before.

'I'll be sensible, I promise,' says Francesca, deciding she'll do something to make Anja happy when she gets back from work. Maybe buy her some flowers. Anja only has the orchids, and Francesca remembers how pleased her own mother had always been when she'd presented her with flowers as a little girl.

OF COURSE he'll be late, thinks Francesca, waiting in the Mauerpark three hours later. How could I expect anything else? She's been told to wait by the basketball courts, and she watches a game unfold. It must be a practice game, she decides, because the teenage players keep breaking off to chat or dance, take a slug of juice or square up to one another. She can hear the music from their old-school ghetto-blaster. Outside the court, a group of four girls are sitting on a grassy bank, gossiping and watching their boyfriends, rolling up their clothes for maximum sun exposure. Every time the boys take a break from play, they seem to inadvertently nod in the girls' direction, as though they don't really want the girls to know they are aware of them watching, but always blow their cover at the very last minute.

Suddenly the world goes dark, and Francesca feels someone's warm hands grab her from behind. She draws breath in shock, ready to kick and scream at her attacker. When the hands release her,

Francesca can't explain why she hadn't known it was just Antonio surprising her, how she'd suddenly lost hold of plausible reality and plunged into a nightmare world where she was being abducted in a park.

'Sorry I'm late,' says Antonio, not noticing Francesca's panic. 'I got this call—'

'Don't worry about it, Antonio,' says Francesca, taking a deep breath and remembering Anja's relaxed response when Antonio had been late for dinner.

'Thanks,' grins Antonio, setting off at a pace. 'I've got something to show you, then we're checking in on Lena, okay?'

'I'm with you all the way, Antonio,' says Francesca. 'Hey, was everything okay with Anja last night? You didn't find it weird getting lumbered with her?'

'*Ne*. She just needed to talk. Her and your parents, they're really good friends, no?'

'Yeah, of course. They were best friends before I was born.'

'I thought so. With you staying there and everything.'

'Well, we didn't exactly plan to. We got chucked out of the place we were renting, where you took me that day, by the lake.'

'So you're accidentally being their guests?'

'Yes, but I think Anja and Richie always wanted us to stay with them,' says Francesca, out of breath. Antonio's powering up the hill and she's doing her best to keep up.

'And your parents didn't want to impose?' Antonio glances behind him and realises Francesca's problem.

'I think so. Or mum just wanted a different kind of holiday. Or something. Actually, I don't think she really wanted to come here at all. It was all dad. He wanted me to see where he was from. He's wanted to come for years, but there's always been something in the way.'

'Well, I'm glad you finally made it, kid.'

Francesca smiles in the sunshine. Antonio has another question, she can tell. Except he's shy of asking it, turning the words over in his mouth while she wills him to let them out so she can catch them. She can't ask it for him.

'Her and Richie, are they happy?'

Francesca is thrown. She didn't think this was about them, about Anja. 'I guess,' she answers coolly. 'I guess they are.' She doesn't mention the card she'd read. Did those words mean they were happy, or not?

Francesca turns to look at Antonio but he's staring further up the hill, his hand over his eyes shielding them from the sun. 'Come on!' he says, grabbing Francesca's hand and pulling him after her. They half run to the top of the hill where there's a wire fence Antonio climbs over. Francesca waits hesitantly on the other side. Antonio's already pulling at the bottom of the fence where the wire's loose. 'You'll have to slide under. It's worth it.' So Francesca drops to her stomach and wriggles from the grassy side of the fence to the bare earth on the other side. She looks around for Antonio, but he's nowhere to be seen.

'Ant-onio,' shouts Francesca, stumbling to the very summit of the hill. 'Ant-onio.' She looks down and suddenly the basketball court and all the people enjoying an ordinary day in the park seem very far away. 'Don't mess around, Antonio, I'm scared.' There's no reply from Antonio and the hill is nothing but a bare earthen mound. He can't have just disappeared thinks Francesca, her heart pounding. It's some kind of test, and she has to think logically. Francesca walks carefully around the edge of the mound, looking down the hillside to see if Antonio's hiding, or, worse, if he's slipped and needs her help. Nothing but a brown paper bag caught on the wire. Francesca sighs and scuffs her trainers against the ground, drawing a faint trail in the earth. WHERE ARE U, she writes with the tip of her shoe. He wouldn't have just abandoned her, would he?

Francesca decides to have one last scour of the

immediate area, then to return to the park, where at least there are other people around. Maybe the reception will be better down there. Typically, the phone she's borrowing doesn't work where she actually needs it.

From the circumference of the mound Francesca starts walking in increasingly small circles, convinced that Antonio wouldn't have played such a mean trick as to have run off and left her up here alone. She's wondering if this is what it's like when police comb a suspected crime scene when she feels something touch her ankle and screams. Looking down, she sees Antonio's blue cap emerging from the earth. Francesca keeps on screaming.

'Hey. Hey. Look, there're steps here. I just wanted to show you the hiding place. It's an old bunker.' Antonio's voice is small from the ground, and Francesca is shaking.

'I'm not stepping into a hole in the ground! Are you crazy, Antonio?'

'I thought you'd like it. Hardly anyone knows about it,' says Antonio, scrambling to stand beside Francesca. 'Just something to add to your tourist's experience. Not many tourists get to see this, though. Not many tourists get to be shown around by me.'

'I'm not just a tourist, Antonio,' Francesca almost yells, surprised at how angry she is. 'I *am* half German, you know. Is that what you think I am? Just a tourist?'

'You're not planning on staying, are you,' says Antonio incredulously. 'You *are* just visiting, aren't you?'

It sounds so coolly logical when Antonio says it, and yet Francesca feels so bound up in the strange things she's found here, and the people she's met, that she wants to be as far away from Antonio's words and the feelings they provoke in her as possible. She stalks to the other side of the mound and sits down sullenly with her back to Antonio and her face in her hands. Antonio watches her without moving, lights a cigarette and sits on the grass, looking at the view over East Berlin.

'My house – is over there,' he shouts across at Francesca, pointing towards an indefinable clump of buildings in the distance.

'Your friends' house – is over there,' he calls, pointing in the opposite direction.

'Tempelhof airport. You see it? – is over there.'

'The lake at Wannsee – you can't see it. But it would be over there,' says Antonio, pointing West.

Silence.

'My uncle's bar – is over there,' says Antonio, gesturing in the distance.

'Okay, I give in – I want to see what you brought me to see,' says Francesca, wondering how long Antonio could cheerfully troop through the sights with no response from her.

'You sure?' he grins. 'There's more.'

'I'm sure,' says Francesca, pulling Antonio to his feet. He keeps hold of her hand as they move to inspect the entrance to the hiding place, a set of stone stairs built into the ground. 'No-one would ever know,' says Francesca in amazement. 'From down there, you'd never know it was here.'

She follows Antonio down the stairs. There's a covering that can be pulled over the entrance, but Francesca shakes her head firmly when Antonio reaches to close it.

It's cold underground, and Francesca wants to have a quick look around and then head back into the daylight, but Antonio is suddenly brooding and won't be moved. He's angry at the graffiti on the walls; that something special like this place has been made shoddy and grimy. Francesca shivers, wishing she'd brought a jumper with her, and for once Antonio doesn't notice.

'Nothing ever stays nice, that's what I hate about the world. Nothing ever stays nice for long.'

Francesca comes to sit beside Antonio on the hard stone ledge. 'Some things do,' she says simply.

'You say that because you're an innocent. And because nobody's gonna make a mess in your world.'

'Well, that's not very fair. I know I was mean to you outside, but that's not fair. Or true.'

Antonio looks at Francesca for a long time, as though considering whether to tell her something. Then he laughs softly, pressing his leg against hers. And before Francesca knows it, they are kissing.

17

Re-treading the journey back to Lena's grandmother's house is strange. This time it's day, but as Francesca and Antonio near Lena's street the sky clouds over and it begins to rain lightly. Francesca once again picks her way across the spongy mattress long ago abandoned in the middle of the street, feeling like she's walking on the surface on the moon. If she returns in twenty years will it still be here, torn and mouldy and stinking of animal piss, marked by thousands of footprints from people who have trodden over it and complained but never stopped to do anything about it?

She hears what sounds like an argument coming from no. 17 – the house with what looks like Christmas lights still up in August. And then she hears laughter, and realises it wasn't a real argument at all, just a TV turned up loud and a window open for summer.

Antonio is beside her, so with the light and the noise and the mattress it's all eerily similar to the scene two nights ago. Except of course it's not the same, nothing ever is. Her and Antonio have kissed for a start. That makes everything different.

But would she ever come back here again, to visit this same street? If it's strange now, imagine how it would it feel to come back in ten years or twenty. Perhaps that's why her mother's acting so weirdly lately. Perhaps the whole city had been to her mother like this street would be to Francesca – somewhere to be closed off and bricked up, never to be revisited.

Antonio grabs her hand and pulls her along to Lena's driveway and out of her thoughts. She can feel the deep grooves in the palm of his hand, and thinks she can hear his heartbeat through their touch. He's pulling her too fast though, and she almost trips.

They're at Lena's door, and Antonio pushes the buzzer and waits. No-one comes, so he presses it again, and Francesca pushes her ear against the grimy glass to try to hear if the buzzer's working. She can't hear anything, so Antonio starts to rap insistently on the pane of glass.

'Be careful, you'll break it,' says Francesca,

looking around nervously. Antonio's making a lot of noise. 'Wait,' she says firmly, squatting down and opening the letterbox to peer through. She can see a pile of untouched mail on the floor. Antonio kneels to get a look too, but she pushes him away with her shoulder. And then Francesca hears something from inside the house, a definite movement on the stairs. Probably too heavy to be one of the cats, but who can tell, she thinks, standing up and backing away from the door.

'She's not in, Antonio, okay? No-one's home. We should go.'

But Antonio's already taken Francesca's spot at the letterbox and is calling Lena's name through it. He's making so much noise he won't hear whoever's in the house. This is a good thing, Francesca thinks. If he thought someone was in there, he'd never give up. She doubts Antonio would stop at breaking the door down if he thought Lena or her grandmother were inside. He'd stomp round to the back of the house and continue making a commotion there.

ANTONIO GIVES one final croak through the letter-box, a last burst of rapping on the door, and comes to join Francesca where she is sitting on a crumbling wall facing the street.

'I don't think anyone's in,' he says.

'I could have told you that half an hour ago,' says Francesca. 'Do you always not listen?'

'Lena said she'd be here. She wanted to see us.'

'Well, maybe she's late,' says Francesca, wondering if Antonio will appreciate the irony. 'If you said you were going to meet someone, like for dinner, you're not *always* there when you say you will be, are you?'

'Lena's not late,' says Antonio, taking his cap off and scuffing his trainer against the wall. *Oh god, it's like he's been stood up or let down by Santa Claus* thinks Francesca, casting around for something to cheer him up. She gives Antonio's hand a tug and attempts to pull him to his feet. At first he doesn't let her, and Francesca tires herself out trying to make him move. She puts all her energy into trying to lift him, but Antonio's far bigger and stronger than her and nothing works.

'Okay, stay there then,' she says finally, giving up. But as she does, Antonio decides it's time to give in, and he's half pulled up, knocking Francesca off balance and somehow managing to head-butt her on the chin. It hurts, but Francesca's just relieved they've made progress. 'So, where are we going to eat then?' she asks. 'I'm starving.'

'I know a place,' says Antonio, perking up. 'There's someone we need to see.'

18

On the way to the snack bar, Antonio doesn't once mention Lena's non-appearance. Nor does he attempt to kiss Francesca again, although to Francesca's mind there is more than one opportunity for him to try. In the empty *U-bahn* carriage for example, when Antonio seemed more interested in telling Francesca about East Berlin before the Wall came down, and how you could leave a bicycle unchained for weeks and it wouldn't get stolen like it would now.

'What, never? You mean there would never be one person who thought it would be a good idea to take someone else's bicycle?' Francesca had replied, unconvinced, her eyes wide and smiling to let him know it didn't matter to her either way.

'Bicycles did not get stolen in the DDR,' Antonio

had said gruffly, standing prematurely for their approaching stop.

And if they hadn't kissed in the empty carriage, maybe they would have embraced when they crossed the little bridge where Francesca had lingered to look at the water running below. 'It's so beautiful,' she had said, ignoring the angry graffiti and the crisp packets bobbing on the surface of the water. 'Don't you think it's amazing, Antonio?' she'd asked, but Antonio had been intent on hurrying her up.

So they hadn't, and Francesca thinks maybe he doesn't want to kiss her again; maybe he hadn't liked it.

Perhaps she should have kept one eye open so she could have checked if he was enjoying it. Of course, it would be okay if he didn't want to do it again. It's not like she's in love or anything. She hasn't even told Charlotte or anyone at school, so no losing face there. That's what's brilliant about holiday romances, Francesca thinks, they can be kept secret and no one has to know if things don't work out. There's zero public humiliation involved.

And then Francesca remembers that it's getting near to the end of the school holidays, and that there is another world and another life waiting for her back at home. Her stomach lurches as she wonders how she'll ever be able to fit back into it.

'We're here already,' says Antonio, placing his hands on Francesca's shoulders. 'It's time you met Jay. And he makes the best kebab in Berlin.'

'Does he do salad?' asks Francesca.

'He'll make you anything you want,' says Antonio, grinning. 'Jay's a genie.'

'A genie?'

'You know – he's like superman in the kitchen. A genie.'

'Oh,' says Francesca, wondering what he means. 'Look – the police are here. You don't think someone's had an accident, do you?'

But Antonio is already bounding on ahead.

'Oy, wait for me!' shouts Francesca after him, breaking into a sprint to match Antonio's long-legged stride.

AT THE DOOR, Francesca is wordlessly waved back by the two policewomen who stand outside Jay's kebab shop like improbable bouncers. She watches silently as Antonio shoulders his way through, and into the shop. Francesca doesn't want to be left outside, but she doesn't know how to even begin to explain why she's here and what right she holds to be inside.

· · ·

So FRANCESCA HAS to make do with watching at the glass front of the shop, peering through the bits that don't have the menu sprayed in large white letters. She stands on her tiptoes even though she doesn't need to. She wants to show the two policewomen who are acting as though she isn't there that she's involved somehow – that she would be inside, doing something, if only she was allowed.

INSIDE, Antonio *is* doing something; he's already at the heart of things. Francesca watches his gestures of anger flash in and out of the white symbols, his arms shaking furiously. She imagines the words he's using to demand Jay's release, mouthing them after him as though she's joining him in prayer. And it can only be Jay, Francesca ascertains, being lifted against the wall right next to the rotating meat in the window by a young and cocky policeman. He must be sure of himself, Francesca thinks, to make such a show of Jay's petite stature like this, holding the little man up so he can't touch the floor, keeping him sweating and spitting like the kebab meat they can all smell, even Francesca and the two police-women outside in the road. To do so in the man's own shop, among his own people – surely Jay has allies here, Antonio for one, and where are the other people that must work here? – Francesca thinks is crazy. Because even though Jay is short, he's bulky, and now that Antonio is looming over him, the policeman seems in danger of losing control.

From the back of the shop, a girl Francesca recognises emerges, laden with shopping bags. She sees again that Lena can only be a year or two older than herself, but looking at her as if for the first time, Francesca feels a much wider chasm between them. Lena's eyes are ringed with smudged black eyeliner and there's a hard, wild look about her.

Francesca keeps her eyes on Lena as she sashays over to the policeman, pausing to rub seductively at a mark she's found on her tight black dress. She stops close to the policeman, close enough, Francesca imagines, for him to feel her mint breath on his shirt when she talks. She doesn't look at Jay, but focuses all the unbearable heat of her attention on the young policeman. Francesca can feel his blush; his desire to shrink from the possibility of her touch.

For there's something about Lena today that's all consuming, that would suck every particle of attention from a room. And for a single traitorous moment, Francesca feels sorry for the young policeman. He's just doing his job, and didn't expect to encounter such a woman – such a force – while doing it.

Besides her, one of the policewomen nudges the

other. Lena's flirtation has not gone unnoticed. The woman taps on the window, apparently unconcerned at the distraction this could cause. She gestures to the young policeman to get a move on, and he finally shoves his charge towards the door and out of it, breaking free of the Lena's spell and ignoring everyone as he bundles a struggling Jay into the waiting car.

AFTERWARDS, inside the shop, the three of them stare at the spot outside where the police car had been. Lena kicks at a table leg, knocking over one of the cheap plastic chairs.

'I don't know what we're going to do now,' she says.

19

Of course, Francesca *can* cook – and this isn't really cooking anyway, it's preparing. Chopping and dicing and splitting, all as Lena dictates, perched high on her stool on the other side of the counter.

Lena is a good manager. Francesca and Antonio are so content to work for her that they never stop to consider whether Jay really does all the jobs she gives them. Francesca works hard for the German girl's acceptance, sensing Lena enjoys making her work hard as she sits looking out of the kitchen window towards the leaking tap outside. It's as if Lena's not sure what Antonio's up to, befriending a girl like Francesca, even if she *is* just on holiday.

'Am I doing it right?' asks Francesca, cutting the

carrots into wonky splintered strips with a meat knife.

But Lena flicks her question away and speaks urgently to Antonio. Francesca watches her pretty nose wrinkle. Suddenly it's desperately important that the older girl doesn't dismiss her as just another waif or stray or curious tourist Antonio's taken up with, without thinking what trouble it might get him in.

'Are you worried?' asks Francesca hesitantly.

'Worried?'

'About Jay, I mean. And your grandmother?'

'Jay will be okay,' says Lena, waving her hand dismissively.

'He'll be back in the morning,' adds Antonio. 'It's the shop Lena was worried about.'

'And now I don't have to be!' smiles Lena sweetly. 'We'll be ready to open like always!'

Lena puts the radio on loudly, probably to stop Francesca asking any more questions. It's the most recent winner of *Deutschland sucht den Superstar*, fronting a vapid song about following dreams, in English of course. *We can have everything we want right here and now, Come with me and I will show you how.* Antonio pulls Francesca to him and dances round the kitchen until Francesca wriggles free.

· · ·

LENA CHATS easily with the customers, shouting frequent instructions from her seat by the window where she lazily chain-smokes menthol cigarettes.

Next to her, Antonio and Francesca have a system: Antonio prepares the meat and cleans his hands to work the till while Francesca dresses the orders in Styrofoam boxes that refuse to stay closed, popping open to show the splurge of sauce and salad and strips of the shop's speciality pita-breads. While Francesca takes the money, counting aloud so Antonio can check it with her, he somehow manages to force the boxes closed until the customer has found a seat, or left the building. The work is fast and busy, but Antonio is good at it.

How do we not feel resentful? Francesca wonders in a quiet moment when everyone is fed and a group of noisy teenage boys have just left the shop, having tried their best to engage her in conversation beyond her immediate sauce or salad duties. We must almost love her to do all this work while Lena just watches, and not mind at all.

HER PARENTS THINK Francesca is kidding when she tells them where she's been. Francesca has never shown the slightest interest in working – not in a café, not in a bookshop, and certainly not in a kebab shop. Of course, Francesca doesn't tell them the full story. They wouldn't like to know she'd only helped out because Jay had been arrested, and that she's determined that beautiful, brittle Lena is going to be her friend.

20

The next morning, before anyone else awakes, Anja rearranges the purple tulips Francesca bought her. They're in a water jug on her bedside table. There were enough flowers to make two displays, and somehow she wanted some of them close while she slept. There's something special about waking up to real flowers, and these are the only unexpected flowers she's ever received. Richie used to buy her roses for her birthday of course, but the ritual has faded in recent years. These days, the only flowers Anja gets are those she buys herself, caught off-guard by a glimpse of a particularly optimistic bloom. While they're fresh, flowers give such a powerful message – that everything is going to be fine, that there's nothing in the world to worry over. After Alexandra died, Anja became a disciple to their teachings, keeping the flat in a constant turnover of the brightest buds: delphiniums, narcissi, and those she chose for their names – paperwhite peonies, avalanche roses, parrot tulips. They made the flat seem peopled. Richie had hardly seemed to notice that they could have been setting up their own flower shop, until one day he'd started sneezing and decided he was developing an allergy and that anyway, he could no longer stand the clash of scents. Anja wasn't to buy any more flowers – it wasn't like they had the money to throw away anyway (although with no child to raise Anja knew she could have argued against this, and won). The truth, though, was that she'd been almost relieved at Richie's interference. She remembers shoving the last of the dead flowers into the dustbin, breaking their necks in one shameful movement.

FRANCESCA'S FLOWERS MARK A DEPARTURE, a step Anja hadn't known she'd taken. All day, Anja had been feeling a fool – embarrassed by her outburst the previous evening. She'd managed to squash it to the back of her mind at work, busy getting the children ready for their monthly assembly, but had been dreading her return to the flat. It *had* been awkward; she'd felt the stranger in her own home, with everyone fussing round, trying to make her feel comfortable. Not saying anything, but she'd known what they were thinking, that all the while they were trying not to upset her, to show they were sorry for not having handled it all better.

And then, ten minutes after her curfew, Francesca had come in garbling an apology, saying something about a kebab shop of all things, and had thrust a huge bunch of flowers into Anja's hands. And suddenly, somehow, that had made it all better. The girl's single act of kindness had taken all the awkwardness and embarrassment of the past twenty-four hours and shuttled it away to somewhere it could be stored for a lifetime without being disturbed.

So this morning, she'd woken to purple tulips and the inevitable comparison she'd been trying to avoid ever since the idea of Imogen, Alex, and Francesca coming to Berlin had been raised all those months ago. Right from the beginning, this child, Francesca, had loomed as much a shadow on Anja's life as her own dead daughter.

The closeness in their age means Anja can't help but look at Imogen's girl and ask: what would her daughter, her Alex, have been like at fourteen? Would she have come home late one day, bearing flowers in apology? Where would they have holidayed together, and what kind of family would they have formed? Would the distance she sometimes feels between her and Richie have been closed by a third part – by the proper family they would have been? Would they have remained a unit – as content with each other as she'd always imagined they would have been – or would something have fragmented them, stopped them from being complete; a happy family? And then the last question Anja always asks, the wall she can never get beyond: what if she'd never met Imogen and Alex at all? What would have happened then?

As Richie groans and turns over in his sleep, Anja repeats her mantra that it's no use picking over old wounds. After all, the three of them will be gone soon, and then everything will go back to normal. She can survive normal.

FRANCESCA WAKES and starts to transform the space from bedroom back to living room. The fish are already up of course, so there's no privacy to laze in bed thinking about the day before. She gives Emilio and Goldie a little wave. Some of the flowers she'd bought are on the table by the window. She's glad she remembered to pick them up from the kiosk at the station on the way home, even if it had made her late. Anja had been so surprised and pleased she'd forgotten to say thank you properly, and later, as everyone had been going to bed, her dad had kissed her on the forehead and told her it had been a kind and thoughtful thing to do. So for once, it seemed as though no one was angry with her.

She can't tell whether it's her good deed, or the kiss she'd shared with Antonio, or even meeting Lena – but all of a sudden Francesca feels very lucky.

For one thing, as self-sufficient and grown-up as Lena had seemed, when Antonio had told Francesca her story on the way home, Francesca had felt sorry for her. 'Lena is a left-over,' Antonio said, and Francesca thought he was making a joke.

'When her parents divorced, they didn't know what to do with her. They left her with her grand-mother, and then they both moved away from the city, and never came back to pick her up.'

'They just left her?' Francesca had asked, wide-eyed. She had friends whose parents had divorced of course, but generally there seemed to be a row over which parent got to keep the children, and how much time they were each allowed to spend with them. She'd thought that was the way it always worked.

'That's what happened. Lena says they had big fights about what was going to happen to the house and their old car, but they just seemed to forget about her. We thought one of them would come back after everything was sorted out, but neither of them ever did.'

Francesca thinks how horrible it would be to be left behind like that, like an unwanted gift, or a child's outgrown toy. But a small voice reminds her of how exciting it would be to be Lena too – in charge of her own destiny, with no-one really to worry about but herself. And of course, Lena has Jay. Francesca had never seen anybody get arrested before, and perhaps because of Lena and Antonio's confidence that he would be home in the morning, it didn't seem such a bad thing after all. In fact, it seemed exciting and romantic. Whatever he'd done, he'd probably done for Lena. Imagine someone loving you so much they'd risk getting arrested for you.

BUOYED up the success of her flowers, and last night's kitchen experience, Francesca decides to pre-pare breakfast for everyone. It's a Saturday, so Anja's at home, and Richie too.

Francesca has no idea what Richie does for a liv-ing, only that he leaves the house later than Anja and seems to have more days off. She does know what he likes for breakfast, though: boiled eggs with soldiers. He also likes to drink a smoothie made with frozen fruit and fresh juice.

So Francesca carefully sets the small table with five places; afterwards pausing to try to force the window open once again. It seems strange to transform the room straight from her sleeping quarters to a breakfast bar. She doesn't *think* it smells, but she can't be sure. She's observed at school that most people have a high tolerance to their own odours.

The window's still stuck, so Francesca rummages in the kitchen for something to take any lingering stench away. The best she can find is furniture polish, which she sprays liberally in the general direction of the settee.

'Not trying to set fire to the place, are you Fran?' asks Richie, passing on the way to the bathroom and poking a dishevelled head round the door.

'And you'd better not be cleaning,' he says, entering the front room on his way back, wearing just his boxers and a crinkled white t-shirt. 'Anja won't have anyone cleaning this place but herself. Me included,' he adds with a wink.

'I'm making breakfast,' replies Francesca, flushing helplessly as she always does when Richie ambushes her. 'I wanted to surprise you. I was going to make a smoothie,' she adds.

'Ah,' says Richie, striding into the kitchen. 'Anja has a very special procedure for that.'

. . .

'I DON'T UNDERSTAND what's happened,' says Richie, scratching his head. 'We make this drink all the time, *kein Problem*. And then I make it with you and look what happens!'

'I don't know either!' says Francesca, staring up at the ceiling smeared with the red and purple remnants of a fruits of the forest frozen mix and the occasional streak of orange.

'*Liebchen...*' says Anja, wandering into the living room and across to the kitchen area, about to thank Fran for the flowers.

She pauses mid-sentence and follows Fran's gaze to the ceiling. A frozen raspberry drops to the floor, bouncing off the lino.

'It wasn't my fault!' says Richie, holding his hands up like a little boy.

Francesca can feel the giggles coming and knows she won't be able to hold them in. She hears Anja saying dryly, 'You two are obviously a bad influence on one another,' before Francesca runs from the room, out of the flat door, and into the hallway where finally she can let go of the laughter. She laughs so much that tears trickle from her eyes, and when her father comes outside to find her he thinks something's really wrong. She's hurt herself, or she's having a panic attack. Francesca can't catch her breath to explain what's happened, so he's still trying to get her to calm down when her mother comes out, hissing: 'Alex, you'll have to see what your daughter and Richie have been up to now. I don't know what's the matter with you lately, Fran; always causing chaos.' She drops to a whisper. 'Look, Fran, can't you see we're living in very cramped conditions here? You need to realise that and try to behave. Or failing that, just try not to make so much mess everywhere – and please especially not on Anja's ceiling!'

Francesca tries to reply to her mother, she really does. But all of a sudden everything seems so absurd that she doesn't think she'll be able to stop laughing, ever. She thinks of Anja's face as she looked up at the ceiling – priceless. She thinks of Richie with fruit all over his hands and staining his t-shirt, looking petrified he was going to be in trouble again, just like the day with the antique canoe. She thinks of her mother trying to placate Anja for the trouble she's caused, and of Anja trying to pretend it's all okay, but everyone knowing it's not.

'I'm sorry, mum,' she wheezes. 'I really am,' she manages to say before another gust of laughter overtakes her.

'Well, *I'm* sorry, Francesca, but I don't believe you,' says her mother, walking back into the flat and slamming the door, leaving Francesca and her father standing in their nightclothes in the communal hallway.

21

'Your mother and I think the three of us should spend the day together.'

'Just the three of us,' her mother repeats emphatically, as though the three of them together is like some kind of magic pill that will stop Francesca being so clumsy and getting her elbows stuck in everywhere, causing problems wherever she goes.

'We thought we could take you to Checkpoint Charlie; you said you wanted to see that, didn't you?' Her father is talking in hushed tones; the door to the spare room her mother and father are sleeping in closed. Francesca can hear the soft whistle of the kettle boiling in the kitchen, and thinks in all likelihood Anja and Richie can hear her father too, so what was the point of bundling her in here, out of sight, and pretending they can't be heard, that there's any real privacy at all, when all five of them know that there isn't?

When Richie had sheepishly let her and her father back into the flat, obviously wanting to apologise but hardly being able to make an apology on behalf of her mother and therefore stuck in an excruciating dilemma of etiquette and left with nothing to say at all, Francesca had seen that Anja had already got to work on the ceiling, standing on a small stepladder to get at the tricky bits with an old piece of cloth. Now there's nothing to be seen, except a slight pinkish tinge if you look really closely, and stare at one spot for an incredibly long time.

Antonio's phone buzzes to let Francesca know she has a message.

'Well, we *could*—' she begins cautiously, ill advisedly letting her reservations show in her voice.

'Ah, do you have other plans, Fran?' asks her mother, archly. 'Because I thought we were here on a *family* holiday.'

'And you wanted to see Berlin, remember?' her father picks up, his tone softer than her mother's but still letting her know she'd better agree gracefully. 'You wanted to learn about some of the history. The Cold War; the Wall. You said you were interested.'

It's true: Francesca had been on her father's side

when he'd been trying to persuade her mother that coming to Berlin for the summer was a good idea; a *fun* idea. Only now she's really here, a visit to Checkpoint Charlie feels like a terribly touristy thing to do. Francesca's sure she already knows far more about the divide between East and West Berlin through the things Antonio has told her than anything she could learn in a museum.

'Or perhaps you'd like to visit the Allied Museum? I remember that's an interesting place; you can learn all about the Berlin Airlift. I visited it the very first weekend I moved here, when I was terribly lonely, right before I met your father.' Her mother smiles for the first time that morning.

'And we could even try the TV Tower for dinner?' says her father, nervously looking from Francesca to her mother for agreement. 'You'll love the views there, Fran. You get to eat in a rotating glass ball, and you can see all over the city.'

Francesca shrugs, then smiles. Her father's right, after all: she may as well agree with grace.

WHEN THE THREE of them are finally on their way, Francesca is surprised to realise what an encumbrance it is to have her parents with her. Her mother had been fussing about what they needed for the day – would it rain, what would they eat; her father gathering guidebooks and checking directions and train times, leaving Anja and Richie with a final apology sticking in his throat. It's so much easier when it's just *me* Francesca thinks, hugging her bag to her on the underground like it's a new secret she's unearthed. And her new life in Germany has taught her that she can look after herself, if only she doesn't have her parents tagging along, taking all day at the ticket machine, an aeon to work out the BVG timetable, and an embarrassingly long time to get themselves settled in their seats.

Her mother's reading an over-priced English newspaper purchased at the station kiosk. Francesca frowns as she watches from her slippery perch of the plastic seats opposite, her mother thinking nothing of unfolding the giant pages over the legs of her neighbour, who's already squashed between her and a large man noisily eating some kind of fish sandwich, the unsociably smelly kind. Her father's keeping an eye on the stops, nervously making sure they don't miss the change, so Francesca finally has a moment to check her message. Her phone beeps as she wakes it from sleep mode, causing the large man with the sandwich to look up momentarily from his food.

JAY NOT BACK...LENA CRAZY.

Francesca wonders what Lena will do. Antonio can't help her all the time – he still has bar shifts to cover. And Antonio had told Francesca there wasn't any money to pay anyone to work, nor was there enough cash to keep the place closed until Jay's return. But perhaps Lena will be able to find herself an endless supply of free labour.

It's their stop and her father looks round at Francesca and alights the train in the anonymous mass of bodies. Francesca almost doesn't make it before the doors close, and for a second her heart is pumping hard as she pushes her way through.

Today, ascending on the steep escalators, Francesca finds it frightens her to be among so many people. We are all so much closer in the summer – an easy target, she thinks with a shudder. This station has something different about it. For starters, there's none of the optimistic advertising to intrude on a person's thoughts, nothing to distract from the naked construction of cold grey concrete, singed as though marked by some ancient fire. She's glad to finally emerge into the open, and hopes they can walk home that evening, and not have to descend back into the underground chasm.

THERE'S a queue to get in to the museum at Checkpoint Charlie, and Francesca doesn't enjoy standing in it.

'We're surrounded by *tourists*,' she hisses in what

is almost a whisper when her father asks what's wrong now. He just wants them to have a nice day together – not a special day – just a good day; a nice day – a day in which they remember they're a family.

'Oh, I see,' he replies. 'But I thought you were on holiday, too?'

'We're visiting. It's different.'

Her mother's look rebukes her. They're standing by the mock checkpoint, where thirty years ago, before Francesca was born, real soldiers would have walked. Today, there are two men dressed in military gear, one with an American flag wrapped around him, the other wearing a Russian flag. People are having their photos taken with the two men, who Francesca assumes must be actors.

It's just all so tacky she thinks, but it's not worth trying to explain this to her parents. Francesca doesn't have time for this shrink-wrapped, sanitised version of history. She can only bear what's authentic. *History through real people* – that would be Francesca's slogan. She imagines splashing the message over the concrete of the naked station.

INSIDE, when she can see through the bodies, Fran stares at the walls of hastily typed translations. This whole place gives the impression of being put together in a hurry, she thinks. As though whoever made the house into a museum had to do so without getting caught, and then they could leave it here, letting the musty secrets of the Cold War escape to a trillion safe-houses.

FRANCESCA HASN'T SEEN MUCH of the Wall while she's been in Berlin, not physically anyway. But she knows it still exists in people's minds; that somehow Antonio and his family feel that the West doesn't belong to them, even now. Each day, they walk the city on one side or other of a wall that no longer exists.

Back in the UK, when she'd been researching the trip Francesca had been fascinated by the photos she'd seen of the Wall. She'd asked her father to tell her about it. They'd made a game of trying to imagine its massive dimensions, and how it had been built. 'What happened to all the concrete, after it had gone?' her mother had asked, and – being an architect – her father had known the answer. 'We've probably driven across it,' he'd answered cheerfully, explaining that the bits people didn't take home for themselves had been ground down and recycled for roads or sold abroad. Francesca hadn't liked to think of that – it seemed as though that material was contaminated; it had di-

vided a city. It seemed wrong to allow it a new identity, in another country. The people there wouldn't
know what they were travelling on, what they were
implicated in. It wasn't fair to them, somehow.

IN THE QUEUE, her mother had said that one of the
reasons Checkpoint Charlie drew so many crowds –
a thousand times more than the Allied Museum,
which she'd take bets on was deserted today – was
that it wasn't just about the sad part of Berlin's history, it was also captured the excitement of all those
thousands of exhilarating attempts to escape to the
West. *That's* what people really wanted to hear
about – the ingenious escape plans, not the people
who died trying to cross a divided city.

Francesca wants to judge for herself why all the
people are here today, why it's important. For once,
she wants to be able to put her mother right at
dinner this evening, one way or another. So she
reads every word of the introduction to the museum
twice, and tries hard not to let the meaning of any of
the translation slip past her and escape unheeded. It
takes a long time for Francesca to read everything
because people keep getting in her way. They walk
right in front of her and block her view. Sometimes
she finds herself moving back to accommodate
them, but after one family shoulder their way in

front of her while she's trying to make sense of a particularly tortured sentence, she vows to stand her ground. In particular, she will circumvent her horribly British habit of saying sorry when she's not at fault.

Finally satisfied she's understood the long introduction, Fran moves to an exhibit of a bruised old suitcase, average size and without wheels. Francesca can't imagine why anyone would own a suitcase without wheels. She knows it's an artefact in a museum, but really – wheels are hardly a modern invention, are they? It gets worse when she discovers the suitcase was intended to smuggle a person – a grown person, and not a child as you might think – into the West. If it had been her, *she'd* have chosen a suitcase with wheels, thinks Francesca smugly. The escape probably failed on that count, that simple detail.

Francesca's about to read on to find out if she's right, when a middle-aged English woman stops square in front of her, calling her little boy over to have him read the story aloud. Francesca can just about cope with having the story read to her by an eight-year-old, but the boy keeps stopping. He's looking over to the other side of the room where his big sister's examining a white car, trying to work out where a stowaway might have hidden. Francesca can see the appeal – he wants the chance to solve the mystery before his sister does; he doesn't want to be practising his reading in front of strangers, and honestly, she'd rather he got his wish so she could finish looking at the exhibition in peace. Unfortunately, the boy's mother is not of the same mind. It's imperative that he reads to the end of the sheet, and properly.

So the boy only gets to look at the car once his sister's jeeringly stabbed her fingers at where the fugitive had lain curled up under the bonnet, doubled up like an intestine, and Francesca loses patience and never gets to find out what happened at the end of the suitcase escape attempt. She follows the trail of the big sister in the next room of the exhibition. This room's quiet – most of the visitors, including the sister, have hurried through it, paying only lip-service to the mass of evidence in front of them, shuffling papers inside their brains but doing no real work.

By the door, Francesca's father stands staring at a blown-up photograph of an old man, his eyes ringed with dirt like a mole's. Francesca knows her dad's waiting for her – he's found something amusing and he wants to share the story with her, like he would have when she was little. He won't call her over to him, but he expects her to come. And she'd like to be able to hold his hand again, and have him explain the story to her, find the joke and present it as though it was only the two of theirs, not public at all.

But to do that would be to read the story backwards, to get the exhibition out of order, and she's tried so hard to keep it all in her head. It'll fall out if she's not careful; she has to do everything just right, like not stepping on the cracks of pavements or eating pudding before dinner, even if she *is* currently in a country where a jam roly-poly is passed off as lunch. Viewing the exhibition in the wrong order, eating dessert before main course – each of these would bleed away at her identity until there might not be anything left.

So Francesca starts at the proper side of the room, and works her way through all the documents and photographs and when she gets to where her dad had stood waiting for her, she is alone, and Francesca suddenly feels sad. Why couldn't she have shared the photo with her father? It's his story, after all, it's why they've come, so the three of them can share her father's heritage between them, her parents' past, offered from one of them to the other like the Quality Street box on Christmas morning. It's just another thing she's got wrong, and she blames the queues of tourists and the summer heat and the selfish woman who got her family in Francesca's way.

Francesca takes a deep breath, and lets herself become submerged in the strange translation. It tells the story of a man in his seventies who'd wanted to escape to the West to join his family. He'd hoped to help with a neighbour's plan, but had been told he was too old. So he'd built his own tunnel with the help of several other men and women of a similar age. Next to his photo is a small print of an old woman in a floral dress being lowered on a wooden contraption down a shaft and into the escape tunnel. It looks like she's sitting on a simple swing, the way a child might, but there's fear in the woman's eyes and Francesca shivers, all of a sudden feeling what it would be like to be truly trapped, to be afraid you might be caught out – and for something a million times worse than anything she's ever done.

'There you are, Francesca!' Her mother's voice echoes in the room, and Francesca jolts away from the picture. She doesn't want to show her mother that the story has spooked her. After all, like all the stories she's read so far, the ending is a happy one. These are the people who escaped. She knows that waiting further in, later in the building, is evidence of those who didn't survive, who might have been shot crossing the death zone, or drowned in a canal or river, or the idea they'd put their trust in. And Francesca wonders whether the visitors who hadn't lingered in this room had stopped at those pictures, mesmerized.

LATER, they eat in the TV Tower at Alexander Platz, high above the city, where Francesca watches the waiters disappear into strange corners as the restaurant slowly rotates. No one mentions the purpose of the day, what they're all here for. It's too brittle to discuss, and instead they take turns to place a small object on the ledge next to the window with its panoramic view, and wait for it to come round again as the restaurant turns. It's the only way of seeing what is moving and what is not.

22

When they arrive back at the flat – late, because her mother had insisted on stopping for another drink on the way home – Richie is watching an old black-and-white film. Anja is out. Richie doesn't say where, and Francesca realises the irony when she goes to ask. Anja's not a teenager, of course, she can go out when she likes, but still, it seems strange that she's not home so late in the evening. If Francesca were Anja, she'd be squashed up to Richie watching the movie with him, her legs casually entangled with his. Richie springs into action when the family come in, but for a second Francesca thinks she'd seen how forlorn he'd looked, and lost.

Everyone seems to have something making them sad, Francesca thinks. Back home, before there had been any talk of making this trip, everything had just worked. She'd read things that made her sad; or watched them on the TV; or thought she knew the feeling herself when things hadn't gone right for her, mainly when she'd found herself in trouble, but never in her life had Francesca seen so many adults make themselves miserable. It had always been the opposite way round – in Francesca's world it had always seemed the adults' job to make the kids miserable – and she'd assumed it was all to keep the adults themselves happy.

Francesca knows Anja is grieving her daughter's death, and it seems to be worse because none of the other adults appear to know how to help her, or even to want to. Francesca's mother has been sulky and miserable because she's been forced to do something she didn't want to, in coming to Berlin. And once here, she's found herself doing other things she hadn't wanted to – like moving in to this flat, and having to join in with everything – even having to come to Richie's birthday party seems to weigh on her. Francesca's father is sad because her mother is making him be, and now Richie, her last hope, has been infected by some kind of melancholy too. But what's driving his sadness? Francesca hopes it is just a momentary loneliness at being left alone for the evening. She wishes they'd invited him along to the restaurant – he'd have laughed at the revolving waiters, even thought of some trick to play on them. She'll have to save Richie, she thinks, and then maybe afterwards he can save her too. But before she can think of what to do, Francesca remembers Lena and Jay, and what she'd felt staring into the dead woman's eyes at the museum. There's sadness everywhere and it's waiting for her, too.

And then for a second, absurdly, Francesca allows herself to ask, what if it's all to do with me? What if *that* was why her mother had fought against coming here – not for herself, but because bringing Francesca here would cause whatever terrible thing was happening?

'FRAN, RICHIE'S TALKING TO YOU.' Her mother passes her a hot chocolate, which burns in the palm of her hand. It's the wrong colour; Anja would have frothed the milk to make the top light and fluffy. 'I think she's tired,' her mother apologizes. 'We all are.'

AFTER THAT, the adults get ready for bed, Richie brushing his teeth first, standing sweetly in the door way with his toothbrush in his hand to say goodnight, as though all of a sudden, with Anja not here, he's the child of the house.

Francesca listens to the noises of the building getting ready to sleep – the clean sound of her mother filling her nightly jug of water, the mush of her parents' whispers seeping through the thin walls, like interference on the radio; the angry flush of the loo before Richie pokes his head round the door to say a last goodnight. Then everyone is settled and the kitchen and the living area changes, becomes Francesca's domain. The light from the fish-tank glows eerily as Francesca looks out of the window and into the street below. She can hear the muted sound of an ambulance siren through the glass. A thought arrives, and she can't push it back. No one had asked. Not one of them had wondered what had happened to Anja. If she'd been knocked down by a car or attacked in a park. If they needed to call the police or the hospitals. Francesca pictures Anja lying bleeding somewhere, thinking of Richie, sure that he'll know something's wrong, sure that one of them will know that something's terribly wrong.

FRANCESCA TRIES her hardest to stay awake, she really does. She stands vigil by the window, holding her eyes open with her hands. She sticks her face into the fridge, hoping the cold will keep her awake. She sits on the floor in front of the fish-tank, as though she's praying to them. *God fish* she thinks, and at this time, in this light, the joke is funny, the idea almost true. Perhaps these five fish really do control the world, thinks Francesca. Wouldn't that be funny? The world controlled from a fish-tank in Richie and Anja's little flat in West Berlin. We'd better all start taking notice of the fish! thinks Francesca, deliriously. Does anyone really know what they're capable of? Goldie swishes past oblivious, and she smiles. Emilio puckers up at the side of the tank. He knows what she's talking about, that she's worked it out. Francesca lifts the lid off of the fish-tank. She waits until Emilio's swimming in her direction. 'Don't worry, I won't tell anyone,' she whispers, watching the ripple effect on the water. She doesn't know if Emilio's heard, so she dunks her head under the water to get closer to him. He swims right past her. *I could just open my mouth*, Francesca thinks, and I'd have the God Fish inside me. She flaps her mouth open three times teasingly, and her ponytail flops into the water and mingles with the seaweed. She hadn't planned to get her hair wet, and Francesca pulls her face up out of the water, scooping up Emilio as she does, leaving a tank tsunami in her wake. She likes the feel of Emilio in her hand, and wanders over to the kitchen to find a tea towel to dry her hair with, pressing her fingers against the fish's body.

· · ·

FRANCESCA HEARS the low squeak of a door. Her parents must be coming to check on her! She hurries to put the top back on the fish-tank. It's heavy, and she imagines the glass slipping from her fingers and shattering into a million pieces on the floor. Could she be like Richie, and hold her hands up to say she didn't do it, walking away from the splinters of glass as though they had nothing to do with her?

She places the roof carefully back on the world of the God Fish and is standing besides it when Anja enters.

'Oh,' says Anja, starting back, as though she's forgotten Francesca is staying.

'You're home!' says Francesca, going to hug Anja as though she's her mother. 'I was worried,' she explains blushingly as they pull out of the embrace. She can't shake the fear that had held her a few moments ago.

'Richie didn't tell you I was out with friends?' Anja asks, looking at her searchingly. Studying her up close, Francesca notices that Anja's complexion is duller than usual, its lustre faded as though all her make-up has rubbed off.

Anja unsteadily pours herself a glass of wine from an open bottle on the sideboard, holding her finger to her lips as though the action is forbidden.

Francesca expects Anja to take the glass and retreat to her part of the flat, to her and Richie's room. But Anja remains standing besides her swaying slightly, as though it's important that the two of them share this moment.

'It must be strange for you here? We must all seem a little strange, no?'

There's a cold edge to Anja's voice that makes Francesca shake her head vehemently. There's nothing strange about staying with some old friends of her parents one summer. Nothing strange in that at all.

'Not really. I like it here,' she says, carefully.

'You should be kind to your parents, Francesca. They are good people. Remember that. We are all good people.' Anja jabs her hand as she makes this point, slopping wine over the light summer jacket she hasn't taken off. She leans towards Francesca conspiratorially. 'Children don't realise the sacrifices their mothers make for them.' Francesca can smell the sweet wine on Anja's breath. It mixes with a cigarette scent Francesca has come to associate with Antonio. 'It's not your fault, Francesca. It's not your fault.' Anja pauses, gives a short bark of laughter. 'But it's not mine either.'

'Oh no,' says Francesca, hurriedly. 'Nothing's your fault. I know that.' It seems important, somehow, to reassure her.

'Because when something is your fault, you should know it. You should say. You should own all your faults, Francesca.'

Simply because Anja seems to be waiting for something before she'll leave, Francesca says, 'I never mean to upset people.' Her confession doesn't seem enough, so she adds, 'I never mean to upset you – or anyone.'

Anja laughs shrilly, and Francesca is scared she'll wake everyone. 'You don't upset me,' says Anja. 'Whatever made you think that? You do get some funny ideas, Fran. You're like a parrot, saying things you don't mean. A little parrot.' Anja drains her wine in one final noisy slurp, and staggers towards the kitchen. That's when Francesca remembers. Emilio. She cuts in front of Anja, says a quick prayer, and places a fine china tea-cup over the tea towel, flipping the fish's body up inside of it. She pours Anja a glass of water from the tap, allowing the sudden gush of water to drown out her thoughts.

AFTER FRANCESCA IS satisfied she is alone again, she slides the glass across the top of the fish-tank and drops in the dead fish. 'I'm sorry, Emilio,' she whispers, closing her ears to the sound of his body hitting the water.

23

For once, Francesca isn't blamed for something, and she wants to be. Richie hardly seems to notice the fish's death, which somehow makes it worse. Emilio was supposed to be his favourite, after all.

Anja is busy making preparations for the birthday party. She's in charge of everything – the guest list, the decoration, of course the food – and she doesn't want anyone's help. Not that Imogen had been sincere in offering, or the men had thought to, but Francesca is genuinely interested in helping with the vodka and tonic sorbets when she sees their tiny plastic moulds in the shape of palm trees and exotic islands.

Her and Anja's night-time conversation had seemed a dream when Francesca had woken the

next day – and the traces had disappeared as
quickly as those of a real dream, rushing though fingers like quicksand no matter how hard Francesca
tried to hold on to them. Anja had acted decidedly
normal, as though she'd never been missing pre-
sumed dead or at least injured the evening before at
all. Perhaps I made it all up, thinks Francesca, but
the ghostly absence of Emilio in the fish-tank re-
futes this.

At any rate, everyone seems to be glad she's
keeping out of the way when Antonio stops by the
flat to pick her up for some adventure or other.
When Antonio's there and Anja's home, Anja always
stops whatever she's doing to talk to him, soon chatting about the bar and his family as though she
knows them intimately. Francesca finds this end-
lessly annoying, and looks pointedly in the other
direction in these situations, boredom oozing from
her pores.

But it doesn't stop with Anja – even Francesca's
father seems strangely pleased to see Antonio,
happy he's keeping Francesca occupied when her
mother's in such a funny mood – one that's getting
worse as the party creeps closer. So Francesca
spends several days drifting between Antonio's bar,
where Antonio teaches her to play darts properly
and introduces her to German rock music; and
Lena's kebab place, where Francesca works away

her penance at what happened to Emilio in contented servitude.

Her and Antonio hold hands occasionally, but nothing more. She tries to send a message to him when she squeezes his hand, but the system seems to have short-circuited, or he's sending back messages she doesn't want to decode. He's warning her not to push it, and Francesca doesn't understand why. He's as friendly to her as ever, and sometimes she catches him staring like he wants to ask her something, but can't. Someone's interfered, she thinks.

Roaming the city with Antonio, Francesca learns there are areas she'd visit with her parents and Richie and Anja that Antonio would never go to. The Wall fell long ago, but Antonio prefers to stick to the East of the city.

Francesca cringes to remember that the first time she'd met Antonio's mother and mistakenly asked her opinion on a West Berlin restaurant she'd visited with her parents. Francesca had known something was wrong – the easy flow of conversation had stopped and Antonio's family had stared at her in disbelief, until Ingrid had taken her aside and whispered that her mother was not in the habit of visiting West-Berlin establishments, so it was no good ever asking her about them.

Her clumsiness has been forgiven, though, and

she's been welcomed into Antonio's big-hearted family. Sometimes, they go to the bar when Ingrid's working, and Ingrid is eager to practise her English and ask about UK cities. Francesca finds she rather likes being seen as an expert in something. The royal family; Ireland; Sunday customs. Soon, when she doesn't know the answer to one of Ingrid's questions, she makes one up.

In contrast, when they visit Lena, she asks nothing about Francesca, who does everything she can to blend in and not offend.

ONE DAY, Antonio has to go to a neighbouring town for part of his mechanic's training, and Lena asks if Francesca will go shopping with her. She wants something new to wear in court; Jay is facing sentencing for breaking into an electronics store and making off with a rucksack full of batteries, after discovering the only TV sets left in there were dummies. Lena's grandmother is at a funeral, so she tells Francesca to come to the house to meet her.

Lena's room is crammed with all kinds of stuff: pyramids of clothes and make-up and shoes, but also old toys and children's books. There's a dusty suitcase poking out from under Lena's bed. It looks as though she'd got halfway through unpacking it a long time ago.

Lena's in the middle of dressing when Francesca arrives, and because she keeps stopping to show Francesca something new – a wardrobe groaning with fifty of her mother's party dresses; a jewellery box her father had given her, the ballerina chipped but turning with a grim determination when Lena sets it going; the largest make-up collection Francesca's seen outside of Boots the chemist – she stays that way for the next hour, the two girls suddenly the same age. Lena roots through dustbin bags full of clothes to find something that might suit Francesca, and soon has her in a dress that makes her look like she's in a music video, complete with earrings so heavy Francesca has to check the mirror to see that her earlobes aren't bleeding. Lena finally finds what she needs to complete her own outfit – a long red skirt that shimmers against her skin. With a feeble attempt to tidy away the evidence of their morning, Lena kicks the bundle of her clothes into the corner of the room, slips her arm through Francesca's and leads her out into the sun-splashed street. A car drives past with its windows down and music blaring out. The driver whistles appreciatively, and the two girls look at one another and laugh like crazy. Francesca's wearing a pair of Lena's shoes, and for once she is as tall as the German girl.

They head for Lena's favourite shop, but a few streets away, she steers Francesca into a low-cost drugstore. Lena deposits Francesca in the make-up aisle, leaving her to browse the two lines of too-bright, sickly-looking make-up. Francesca's soon bored, and aches to be outside in the sunshine, but it seems strangely disobedient to stray from the spot Lena had left her. It's as though she's a small child waiting for her guardian to come back, and she stands on tiptoes in Lena's painfully high shoes, scanning the building for the older girl. At her second sweep of the room, she spots Lena's curly hair bobbing up and down right at the other end of the shop, where Francesca sees there is a small per-fume counter.

Francesca knows there's something wrong about the picture even before she can take it all in. Lena leaning too close to the dark-haired man, his syn-thetic shirt slightly too tight, the cheap advertising display looking as though it's about to fall on them. And then she realises. It's Richie. Her Richie. Anja's Richie.

She approaches them slowly, dipping behind each aisle as though she's part of a SWAT team: Sunglasses; Bathing products; Hair Colouring kits; twenty-six different brands of Mouthwash. The pair come into full focus, Richie's hand lightly holding Lena's wrist as he puffs a new scent into the air. The smell is overpowering: sharp, too many things at once, all trying to lead in different directions – like an untrained orchestra playing without a conductor. So this is where Richie works, where he's been on those missing days – selling perfume to girls like Lena. Francesca had never thought to see Richie in this neighbourhood, let alone discover this is where his employment is. Lena looks suddenly in Francesca's direction, and Fran thinks she's caught. She holds her breath, trapping the prickling cloying scent in her mouth. Lena is telling Richie who she's with, that someone's waiting for her. Not a friend, just 'someone', and taking this to confirm Lena's in no hurry, Richie searches for another perfume to tempt Lena with. This one's the most expensive: it's locked in its own tall glass cabinet, and when Richie holds it to the light Francesca can see tiny specks of gold sunk to the bottom of the emerald bottle.

Francesca wants to slap her then, to drag Lena away from the counter and all the way back to her bedroom slum in her miserable grandmother's house.

Instead, Francesca watches, hypnotised, as Richie and Lena search for a virgin patch of skin. Her wrists won't do; there are five different per-fumes competing there already. The front of her neck shows a gleaming trail in the store's cold light: three summer scents mingling there. So Lena slowly turns, like the dancer in her jewellery box, sweeping up her auburn curls to expose the nape of her neck.

Francesca has the sickening sense that she's watching a ritual, and all at once her irritation, the unfairness of it all, won't be held. She steps forward into their world, breaking it into a million pieces.

RICHIE COUGHS, colours, looks uncomfortable, while Lena spins round accusingly, her hair still held high above her head.

'What are you doing here? I told you to wait at the make-up counter!' She's made herself bigger than Francesca again, too large for this shop, this scene, goddess-like.

'Fran, you know Lena?' Politeness has crept in with a mask to offer, as though they're already at his birthday party and Richie is playing host.

'This where you work, Richie?'

'Yes, pathetic, isn't it? I wouldn't even buy this crap.'

Lena lets all the weight of her hair drop and Francesca is relieved to see she's returned to her normal stature. Her aura has withered to a pea with the hurt of Richie's words, and in seconds Lena is just an adolescent girl again. She puts down the bottle she had been preparing to purchase. After Lena informs Richie that her and Francesca have to go, Francesca almost expects her to add 'Loser', like some of the girls do at school when they've been stung by some boy they like.

'I'll see you tonight, Richie.' Somehow, Francesca knows they are both looking at him with betrayal in their eyes.

24

Later, when Francesca sees Richie back at home, fussing around Anja, listening to her menu for the party with more than usual patience, she knows everything has changed between them. She's seen his weakness, like a wife who's watched her husband when he didn't know she could be looking.

And from that evening, Francesca knows she's really there for him; suddenly what she says matters. He asks a question and wants to know what her answer would be; for the first time Richie looks at her properly when he speaks to her. She exists for him in a way she never has before. Turning it over in her mind, Francesca knows that whatever it was, that small scene at the chain-store perfume counter has upset the balance of their relationship, and brought Richie closer to her. For the moment, the feeling is delicious. So delicious, she can almost forgive Lena her part, her bewitching ways.

It has come easy, this forgiveness, for Francesca had found that the best salve to her pain had been to not stop talking about Richie. She wanted Lena to know about all the days they had spent together; the mornings they both wake before the rest of the house and Richie finds a newspaper article to teach her German from; that her dad was Richie's best friend; that it was Richie's birthday tomorrow and she, Francesca, would be at the party. Lena would not – unless Francesca bestowed her the favour of an invitation. Francesca has learnt that it is easy to forgive when one wins a substantial increase in power.

Her mother is acting as though everything is normal, but Francesca knows she is sitting on the edge of hysteria. She is concerned about the guest list. Francesca knows this because three times she has asked Anja to list everyone who is coming to the party, and each time Anja has given the same breezy reply – 'old friends and new'.

Francesca has watched her struggle to control her impatience. She's used to having all the information she needs at her fingertips. In her mother's normal world, she has two ever-diligent assistants paid to answer her queries, to provide her with all the research she needs to make sure everything she's in charge of runs smoothly. Right now, she wants to know exactly who's coming tomorrow so she can make sure everything runs to her plan, but just as Lena couldn't bring herself to ask for what she really wants – an invite – Francesca's mother can't bring herself to ask again for what *she* really wants – to know which of their old acquaintances she'll have to face tomorrow. And Francesca knows that Anja is enjoying tormenting her mother just as much as Francesca has enjoyed tormenting Lena.

FRANCESCA IS SITTING on one of the high bar stools at *The Happy Giant*. There are no customers, and Antonio's uncle is out the back checking through the day's takings. If she tips her seat forward and looks to the left, she can just see him counting a small wad of notes over and over again, muttering to himself as though he doesn't trust his own sums.

'I should be here tomorrow,' Antonio says, finally filling the pause after he hears Anja has extended an invitation to Richie's party. 'Gus might need me.'

From the back room comes the sound of Uncle Gus chuckling. Francesca knows what he means. Antonio only has to look around the empty bar to see he's not needed today, and most likely won't be needed tomorrow, or the next day either. She wonders what she's done wrong.

'I have a good feeling we might be busy tomorrow. My friends are coming over.'

Gus sighs; like Francesca, he knows Antonio's generosity with his friends is part of the problem.

'I should be here,' repeats Antonio, with his stupid dog-like determination, refusing to meet Francesca's eyes.

So FRANCESCA never gets to explain to Antonio that she needs him at the party, that she needs a friend to help her deal with her mother's mounting hysteria. After today, she knows Lena can't be the friend she needs. And now Emilio's dead she doesn't even have the fish to talk to. As she tries to sleep, all she can see is Goldie swimming past, looking at her reproachfully through the glass.

That night, Francesca dreams she's sitting an exam. After spending months revising for all the possible options, when she turns the paper over, there's a picture of Emilio, although he's all the wrong colours, painted lurid, and only one question: **Does killing a fish make someone a murderer? Discuss, making reference to your own ideas and personal experiences.** In the dream, she doesn't know where to start. Billions of people eat fish every day. Are they all murderers? She killed Richie's fish. Is she a murderer? Then she remembers the charge of manslaughter, the accusation of negligence, and writes three whole paragraphs on that, in her neatest and most even handwriting. And then, finally, she can rest.

25

The next morning, Francesca wakes to find a rock of dread has settled at the bottom of her stomach. She tries to shift it to make room for her breakfast, but can't. Instead, she picks at a few of the shrivelled purple grapes that have spent the past four days partially transforming into raisins in a bowl by the window. She hopes no one will notice her loss of appetite, but instead they all seem to be hiding from the sun that is streaming in through the unopened window.

Imogen has procured some information about the airport attack her and Francesca had narrowly missed. She wants to chew it over with someone, the way they would be doing in the newsroom, to look at the attack from every aspect, to check every link the fresh morsel of knowledge offers. She offers the information like it's a juicy bone: the attack was one of three that were planned, but for reasons unknown the other two were never attempted, although two mysterious dead bodies were found near to both locations. The news that the other attacks would have been on a busy shopping centre and a central bus station is met with silence, and even as Imogen expounds on the implications of the two locations – the probable scale of blood if both attacks had been carried out as planned, she suspects that no-one is really listening, not even her husband or her daughter. She trails off, huffing in despair at their dull disinterest. Once, she had expected great things of her daughter.

Anja can't help exhaling in relief when Imogen stops lecturing them – she doesn't know what Imogen expects them to say. Anja firmly believes that it's dangerous to pay too much attention to the news. She'd rather leave it to run itself out in the background where it belongs. Terrible things are happening all the time, and she's not in the habit of dissecting them over breakfast. There's always more news, and once you start trying to unravel it, you'll probably never stop, until one day you might lose your mind. Of course, to someone like Imogen, it's all just a soap opera – the whole world there to be gossiped over.

Francesca wants her mother to stop talking

about the attack too. It's not helping to lift the rock in her stomach at all, and Francesca knows it'll just make her mother itchy for work, for somewhere she knows she's important, where there are hundreds of decisions for her to make each hour of the day. If her mother doesn't calm down, soon she'll be taking it out on all of them, and it's poor Richie's birthday today. Unusually, he's not up yet, and Francesca makes a quick atheist's prayer that he lies in a little longer, so that there might just be time for the mood to shift before he joins them. She can't bear to think his birthday might be ruined.

When Richie comes in, he teaches Francesca the words to Happy Birthday in German, and then they all sing it together, with Richie and Francesca singing the loudest – him singing along to his own song to help her follow. 'Ach, it's just the rehearsal,' he says, when Imogen admonishes him for joining in.

Her mother looks pale this morning, and through the day Francesca catches her looking queasy. Francesca almost expects her to cry off the party sick, but then where would she go? Imagine what everyone would say if she decided to check herself into a hotel! Imagine if they had to cancel the party for her! Perhaps it would be too late to get hold of everyone, and some people would turn up expecting a party, which Francesca's mother had sabotaged.

Somehow, they make it through to five o'clock, which is the earliest Francesca has decided she can put on her new red dress. She tiptoes into Anja's room, and across to her wardrobe, easing the door open slowly so it doesn't squeak. There it is, waiting for her. She bundles the fabric out of the wardrobe, slips into her parents' room, and puts the bolt across. She holds the new dress out to the mirrored wardrobe, as though she's offering it up to the mirror gods, in silent prayer that the dress will look as good on her today as Anja and the shop assistant had persuaded her it would the day she'd bought it.

She undresses, and pulls the material over her body in one go, scrunching her eyes closed. She loves the feeling of brand new clothes. When she opens her eyes she practically purrs with approval. For once, everything looks right. She's still admiring herself when the door handle turns and she hears her father asking if she expects him to get ready in the hallway. 'Good idea!' she says, teasingly, listening to him do so while he tells her if anyone walks in on him it's all her fault. She takes one last look at herself before she unbolts the door.

'Nice tie dad,' she says, glad he hadn't minded the indignity of dressing in the hallway.

'Thank you, Fran.' He casts a quick glance at his

attire in the wardrobe mirror. 'You look nice your-self.' As he starts to leave, Alex turns to look at his daughter properly. 'Although, isn't that dress a little revealing? I haven't seen you wear that one before.'

'It's just a backless dress, dad. Anja helped me choose it.'

'It suits her,' says Anja, appearing in the doorway like a ghost, Francesca's mother following, no doubt curious to see her daughter in the dress Anja had shopped for with her.

'I was just saying how grown-up it makes her look,' says Alex, squeezing past Anja in hasty retreat.

'Poor Alex,' says Imogen, looking at her daughter in the mirror, 'he doesn't know how to handle it.'

'Handle what?' asks Francesca, blushing at the scrutiny.

'You growing up!' reply Imogen and Anja in uni-son, for once the tension between the two women breaking.

'CLOSE YOUR EYES, RICHIE,' says Anja, turning out the lights. There's a hush before a passable rendi-tion of 'happy birthday' is sung by Richie's assorted friends and loved ones. *Zum Geburtstag viel Glück.* Francesca picks out the words carefully, trying her hardest to get them right for Richie. His eyes are closed, and she hopes when he opens them, he'll be looking straight at her, and he'll see everything she wishes for him. The thought makes her giddy.

WHEN RICHIE OPENS HIS EYES, his first impression is that there are too many candles on the cake – so many, they might set light to the house if Anja's not careful. She's holding the cake out in front of Richie, waiting for him to blow out the flames.

'I'm not that old,' he grins, 'there must have been a mistake.' He takes a deep breath. Growing up, it had been the tradition in his house to have to blow out all the candles at once. They'd built it up so much that one year his little brother Luis had run from his birthday party crying when he hadn't been able to manage it. Today, the candles flicker, but when Richie sucks in his breath they come alight again. Richie takes another deep breath and blows as hard as he can, concentrating on reaching all the candles. This time he's got it, he's completed the test. He's not so old he can't blow out his own candles. Richie smiles at Anja in relief. His friend Martin from Sunday afternoon football slaps him on the back. Richie looks back at the cake, one from the supermarket with a blown-up picture of himself on it, and sees the candles have come alive again. This time he quickly takes a really gigantic breath and expels the air in one big circular motion over the cake. His friends clap. The candles go out, and then re-ignite. Richie swears, gets ready to try again.

'We got you!' says Anja, removing the cake from Richie's reach. Richie feels foolish, and a fool for his mounting annoyance.

When Anja brings the cake back in from the kitchen, this time the picture is cut into pieces. Richie remembers the photo being taken, on holiday at his parents' place. He's pulling a silly face, trying to make Anja laugh. Richie takes a piece of his birthday cake – a cross-section of his tongue and cheek – gives Anja a big, showy, kiss and turns the music back up.

Francesca watches as Richie invites her mother to dance, pulling her around the room so fast it makes her laugh. Martin and his new wife join them. Francesca feels giddy, and wishes it were her Richie were dancing with, or at least that she could make herself join in. A year ago she would have. They would have all danced together, her dad too, like they had at New Year. But somehow in the months in-between, something's changed, and to-day, in her new red dress, nothing would make Francesca join her mother dancing.

Anja had issued the invitations to the party, so everyone is a mutual friend of her and Richie's. 'Old friends and new,' as she had explained to Imogen, fanning her distress. Three or four of the men Richie used to go drinking with, most of the Sunday football crowd with their wives and girlfriends, a man called Harry who Richie has not seen socially for several years, but whose telephone number Anja still had for some reason she can't recall. He's late arriving, and Anja thinks he probably won't come after all. It doesn't matter; she'd only invited him on a whim, remembering a funny incident when they'd all gone to the lake at Wannsee together. Imogen and Alex had been there, it hadn't been long before they'd got together; and Harry; and some others Anja can't remember. They'd taken a large pedalo out, like you could then, and had stayed out on the water drinking and picnicking past their time. Harry thought the girl at the base wouldn't mind; he swore he'd be able to persuade her not to take the penalty from Alex's bankcard. He'd wanted to show off how charming he was, Anja supposed. He *had* been very good-looking. Somehow, that day, Alex had ended up pushing Harry into the water with his clothes on, or had it been the other way round? Anyway, someone had ended up getting wet, and remembering that had made Anja laugh and had made her invite Harry to this party. She doubts Imogen and Alex will even remember him. She doubts he will turn up at all.

.   .   .

FOR FRANCESCA, the novelty of her new dress is beginning to wear off. She'd started the evening feeling surprisingly pretty. Usually, Francesca chooses her clothes with one thing in mind: to blend in, but when Anja told her to try on the backless dress, Francesca knew for once what it felt like to attract attention rather than hide from it.

But now, everybody's talking so fast and laughing so much, that Francesca's beginning to feel like a complete outsider. Her mother is engrossed in conversation with Martin's bossy wife, Monika. Francesca knows she's bossy from the short conversation she'd been accidentally caught in about Francesca's future career plans. For no reason Francesca could think of, and in the space of approximately three minutes, Monika had determined Francesca should train to be a doctor, which was exactly the kind of idea Francesca *didn't* want her mother getting. Monika had also jokingly told her mother she should keep an eye on her father, who wasn't getting any less devastatingly good-looking with age. Francesca found the sentiment disgusting, and couldn't believe Monika's rudeness, but surprisingly her mother hadn't been at all bothered and has been chatting with the woman all night.

In the middle of the room, Francesca's father

and Richie are bouncing jokes and one-liners off of one another for the entertainment of an ever-changing circle of old friends. Overhearing another punch-line, Francesca has to admit they are a very funny duo, and Richie looks doubly gorgeous in the new shirt Anja gave him just before the party.

Anja walks over from the kitchen to join the group gathered around Richie and Alex. As she waits for someone to move and let her in to the cir-cle, Francesca realises Anja's probably the only person at the room feeling less comfortable than she is. She always seems to be checking things, smoothing table covers, or fetching another drink at twice the rate anyone else needs a re-fill. And now that they are surrounded by other people, Francesca notices that her mother and Anja's paths barely cross, although at points they each gravitate towards the group in the middle, where Alex and Richie are holding court. It is as though they are two planets orbiting the same sun.

SITTING SQUASHED up on the sofa by the door is a man called Harry who smiles at Francesca every few minutes. Francesca had seen him slip into the party later than everyone else, let in by the wife of one of Richie's friends, his entrance barely noticed. Francesca can sense he's biding his time to come over and talk to her, but this just makes her nervous. She won't say anything that makes sense, and it'll be obvious how young she is, that she's waiting to see how late her parents will let her stay up. She flushes with embarrassment, imagining her mother breaking up the party early, just so Francesca can get to bed at a decent hour.

Anja's made the room look nice – it's softly lit with some special lamps Francesca hasn't seen before, and there are candles burning by the fish-tank, reminding Francesca of her shame. She scratches at a scab of unknown origin she's found on her arm, and pushes Emilio off the cliffs of her mind.

It's hot, and when Francesca sees Harry get up from the sofa and begin to make a beeline for her, she turns to the large window and tries to open it. It's stuck, and after pushing harder, Francesca realises the window is painted shut. How strange she thinks, to have such a nice big window and to paint it shut.

'You're not having so good a time?' Harry has made his approach. 'I find grown-ups very boring myself.'

Francesca doesn't know what to say to this. She notices her father watching them slyly from the other side of the room, ready to abandon the conversation he's leading. Her mother is on alert too, leaving Monika in mid-conversation to whisper something to her father. She looks panicked, which Francesca thinks is funny. Why shouldn't she talk to this man if she wants? No-one else is bothering with her.

'It's a nice party,' Francesca says. Harry has to lean towards her to catch her words.

'I hear you're staying with Richie and Anja?'

'Yes,' Francesca smiles, trying to think of something more interesting to say.

'I've been admiring your dress. It's a good colour for you.' As he looks at her intently, Francesca changes her mind about wanting to be noticed. She looks away awkwardly.

'You don't need to worry about me; I'm an old man and I knew your parents before. Your mother was very pretty, and very *free* – yes, that was what I liked about her. What we all liked about her.'

'You're looking tired, Fran,' says her father, appearing next to Harry. 'It's probably time you went to bed.'

'Oh no, I'm not tired,' says Francesca quickly.

'Who could sleep with all this going on?' asks Harry. 'Harry Rosenfeld, an old friend of Richie's,' says the man, thrusting his hand out for Alex to shake. 'We met, once. At the lake.'

'Funny, I don't remember you,' says Alex bluntly, and Francesca cringes at her father's rudeness. 'If you don't mind, I need to borrow my daughter.'

'Of course. It was a pleasure to meet you, Francesca.'

Francesca smiles at the stranger gratefully; he has more grace than her parents with their crazy manners lately.

FRANCESCA CAN'T WAIT ANY LONGER. There's someone talking in the bathroom, and she needs to go. Desperately. It's not like there aren't four other rooms to chat in. She pushes the bathroom door open a fraction. To her surprise, she can just see her mother through the sliver. It's like watching a tiny part of a TV screen while everything else is static and fuzz.

Her mother is holding on to the side of the bath to stop herself shaking. Francesca listens as her mother implores Anja to make one of Richie's guests leave the party. Her words drop from her lips like pebbles. She thinks Anja is punishing her; that there's something to be punished for. Her mother can hardly breathe and Francesca wants to run in and help her, to pull her out into the fresh air where they can be alone.

'I know you might want to hurt me, but what about them? You don't know what it's been to keep us together all these years. What it took in the beginning, when we first left.'

'*I* didn't do anything, Imogen. None of this started with me.' There are tears in Anja's eyes, and Francesca believes her. She hadn't meant this.

'Perhaps we can't control it forever, Imogen.' And then Anja walks into the sliver of light Francesca is watching. Her face is gentle, and she pulls Francesca's mother into her and holds her as she sobs, rocking her back and forth as though this will calm her.

'We have to leave,' Francesca's mother says repeatedly. 'Harry knows, I'm sure of it. He saw us at the lake. Always hated Alex. He'll think nothing of—' She gulps air, her body shuddering. 'I'm taking my daughter, and we have to leave *now*.'

WHEN FRANCESCA MOVES AGAIN her body feels old. She has been holding her breath without realising it, and somehow she feels as though a trick has been played on her – as though she's been playing musical statues with her eyes closed, and she has opened them to discover all the other children have snuck away. She knows what she has to do. She must find that man again, and talk to him. She needs to know what caused this so she can make sure it doesn't keep upsetting her mother like this. She can't forget how fragile her mother looked; how she'd broken, with Anja holding all the pieces together.

Francesca runs to the kitchen, scanning for Harry among the faces there. She expects to find him in the hallway by the door, to be able to catch him as he's almost leaving. She expects he'll make her jump when he's the last person she looks at, when she's almost given up. Her father is talking at the centre of a group. She waits for his attention.

'Dad – where's that man?' He has to bend down to hear her properly, so it's like they're playing Chinese whispers but she finds she can't whisper. 'That man who was talking to me – where is he?'

Her father frowns. 'Harry?'

'Yes – where's Harry?'

'I don't know. I think he left.' His English sounds impatient. He wants to get back to his German world, thinks Francesca, bitterly. Perhaps that's where he feels he belongs the most. *But what about me*, she thinks. *Where do I belong now?*

'It doesn't matter,' she says, thinking she hasn't searched the bedrooms. Perhaps he's still looking for his coat. Perhaps Anja had hung it at the back of her wardrobe, in the spot where Francesca's dress had been waiting for today, and had neglected to tell anyone. She walks bravely into the room, and flings open the wardrobe door, with the false hope that lovers can sometimes carry. Nothing. Just a wardrobe crammed with a hundred disguises and a slight gap where her dress had hung. She runs her hand across the different fabrics, trying to feel all the different sensations in one go, until the gap is no longer there and it's all just one big mess.

Afterwards, she goes quietly to Anja's dressing table and opens the drawers one by one. Everything is arranged neatly. There's one drawer for underwear – the silky kind Francesca has seen pictures of in magazines but would never dare buy for herself; another for make-up – expensive and well looked-after; and in the third, among Anja's jewellery, Francesca finds what she is looking for.

And then she waits, holding her breath, and jabbing the pin from Anja's silver butterfly clip into the palm of her hand; she waits in the cupboard with the door open, until she hears first her mother and then Anja softly close the bathroom door. She counts to one hundred and fifty to make sure neither her nor their cover is blown, and then she goes into the bathroom, where the ghosts of her mother and Anja's conversation await.

She sits on the toilet for the longest time.

26

F rancesca feels empty. Everyone has left; the party's over; and Harry never came back, is never coming back. Her mother and Anja are strangers to her. They'd returned to the party and acted as though nothing had happened, as though things were as normal as they ever could be between two women who are no longer friends. Below it all Francesca feels a vortex whirling, another life they might all fall through into, if only she had the courage. If only she were brave enough to tell her mother what she'd overheard, and if only she had the power to make her mother listen to her. Right now, she knows that if she confronts her mother, hauls her out of bed like her mother would if she'd discovered Francesca had done something wrong – somehow, she'd still be invisible. She'd be imagining or exaggerating, and she'd never be admitted to the hallowed halls of truth.

She wonders what the truth would look like. She'd tried to draw it once, for one of the comics she used to make when she was a child. She'd drawn truth as a shining gold egg. A shining gold egg, with something unknown inside waiting to hatch. Maybe the truth has to be fed every day, she thinks, or it'll wither away and die.

Francesca hadn't been one of those children who'd found it easy to tell a lie. Until the age of thirteen, she'd agonised over where the boundaries between fact and fiction lay. How she'd hated being at school when one of her class had done something wrong. She felt implicated just by being there, and not speaking the truth. And then one day she realised, speaking about her parents on the phone to her grandmother, that as soon as you took more than one person and tried to tell the truth for them, it didn't work. There wasn't one truth, and answering almost any question about someone else resulted in a lie. She tried to talk about the revelation with her father, but he just looked confused and asked her if her grandmother had been trying to cause problems again. Francesca had thought it was no wonder her parents argued all the time about who said what and when, if they couldn't grasp this simple rule.

Her mother had spoken a lot about truth when Francesca was growing up. Not home-truths, domestic truths, whether Francesca lied about washing her hands, but the Big Truths she was always hunting at work, the kind of truth that had to be chased relentlessly and treated brutally when it was won. She hated to let a story get away, to let the truth fester unfound. Perhaps we all do that with truths that are not our own, thinks Francesca. Our own truths are what we hide from.

And perhaps it *is* better if the truth can be ignored until it dies: she'd never admit to anyone how she sometimes feels for Richie, and maybe, if she's lucky, the truth will expire before anyone notices. Even now, alone in the dark, she can feel her face burning as she thinks of the horror of anyone discovering *her* truth: that somehow, secretly and most definitely accidentally, she might just be in love.

She'd known it when she'd seen him with Lena, just as she'd known that although Lena might think she's in love with him too, for Lena it's just an infatuation that will soon light on some other man at some other counter in some other cheap store. Yes, it was pathetic that Lena had believed anything real existed between her and Richie – someone who, after all, was just the man at the perfume counter, paid to disguise the coldness of commercial transaction.

But to Francesca, Richie was real, and now, thanks to Lena, Francesca was real to him too. She was winning.

WAKING the next morning is difficult. Francesca can feel the day-time world speaking urgently to her, offering a hand to tug her free of the tangle-weed of dreams that holds her fast, loosening slowly to let her glimpse the bright white freedom of day, before forcing her back down into the muggy depths of sleep, where the strangest thoughts await her. She is struggling to work something out; the words Love and Forgiveness light up like words on a billboard; Alexandra is there, imploring her to deliver a message, but she speaks so quietly Francesca can't catch the words, and soon Francesca's crying in frustration, her tears tiny orange goldfish which she watches swim away into the daylight that dances on the surface of sleep. There's a beautiful green mermaid dress, so perfect it makes her forget all about helping Alexandra, and as Francesca stands looking at it longingly, it arranges itself on her body, forging its pattern onto her skin so she thinks she'll never be able to take it off. And then kneeling in front of her expectantly is Richie, holding a bottle of her mother's favourite perfume, which he is offering to puff erotically onto her neck. Her mother and father are together, sitting on edge of the little bed she had as a child, telling her the story of Thumbelina in tandem. Richie grins and squirts the puff of perfume in her eyes. Love and Forgiveness, she thinks. And then the words she's been searching for settle into place:

You ask for me to forgive you, but I can only love you, and wait for you to forgive yourself.

She remembers Richie's writing, the tails of his letters long and feminine. And then Harry arrives in the taxi that brought them to the wrong street, calling from the window for to her to wait, while her father orders her to come away immediately; and Alexandra is there, imploring Francesca to deliver a message she can't hear; and she's crying orange goldfish; her mother is asking her what happens at the end of *Thumbelina*, but she can't remember; and she wants to take the mermaid dress off but it's part of her; and she can feel the dress burning her skin, and the perfume stinging her eyes; and if she doesn't do something quick she thinks she's going to drown. Love and Forgiveness. Love and forgiveness. She repeats the words as though they will save her, and then Antonio is in front of her, bowing low and guiding her home. *Say it like this!* he says, cutting away the seaweed with his penknife and leading her free into the daylight.

SHE BLINKS. Her mother is staring down at her, a bundle of Francesca's belongings gathered in her arms. Francesca's silver trainers are squashed next to the diary she's been keeping, and the little bag of postcards and souvenirs her father had bought her at the TV Tower is nestled next to her new red dress, crumpled and unwashed.

What's wrong she wants to ask, but Francesca knows what her mother will say before she says it: Something's come up. We have to leave. She wants them out of there today, and while Francesca's been sleeping, she's already booked the flights. Her mother will have an excuse, and Francesca doesn't have to believe it.

THE EARLIEST FLIGHT her mother could get is not until the evening, and so Francesca has a full day to think up her own plan. She's not ready to leave Berlin yet. Richie is in her bones like a fever, and she has to speak to him alone. There will be a sign, and she'll persuade him to let her stay, and if her parents won't agree they'll run away together, to Vienna or Spain, where Richie can be back where he belongs in *his* home, and soon she'll belong there too, and all traces of her former life will slowly be erased. They'll drink sangria every morning and each day they'll drive through dusty whitewashed villages on a little orange moped, which is the only thing they'll need to own. They'll swim every day in the bright blue sea, and she'll learn to speak Spanish properly, in the beautiful singsong way Richie does.

And so Francesca is able to wait. She waits while Anja tidies around her from the party, and her mother busies herself getting ready for the family's abrupt departure. And as she waits Francesca is able to make-believe a calmness at the decision, an acceptance of the turn of events. Her mother even comments on how mature she is being; how she'd thought Francesca would cause a fuss at leaving her new friends so suddenly. She promises a trip back to Berlin later in the year, but when Francesca looks at her father's face she knows neither one of them believe it.

Her father isn't fighting either, and Francesca wonders why. Perhaps her mother's excuse really is watertight. Perhaps he just doesn't care.

Francesca notices with pleasure that Richie is solemn today. He's definitely sad at the idea of their leaving. She just needs the opportunity to speak to him alone, an opportunity that doesn't come up often in this tiny, claustrophobic flat.

She must find time to see Antonio before the end of the day, too. She's not sure what it was between them, but to leave without saying goodbye would be wrong, like uprooting a young tree and leaving it to rot in the city. She can't speak about her plans with Richie – imagine if he told Lena – and already Francesca knows that outside this day, she won't talk to Antonio again. He belongs to these last weeks – to those long, light days, and nowhere else. There won't be messages or phone-calls or plans for future visits.

Her mother chatters deliriously about the arrangements of the flight, and getting home, and Francesca's first day back at school, but Francesca ignores it all, safe in the knowledge that, this time, she won't be on the flight. She tunes out her mother like she's learnt to tune out the circling of bees at the painted window. Neither can hurt her.

AN HOUR or so after breakfast, Richie says he needs to go to the shop to get something for his head. Francesca takes this as a signal and is about to get ready to go along too, when her father muscles in. He could use the air, he says, and Francesca could scream. Richie had engineered the perfect opportunity for them to be alone together, and her father has ruined it. She sits and sulks, while Anja cleans around her and her mother busies herself checking everything's ready for the trip. As she dusts off the tiny television, Anja tries asking Francesca about her plans for the new term, and Francesca suddenly feels sorry for her. After all, Anja has no clue what they are planning, Richie and her: they are about to destroy Anja's world.

ON RICHIE and her father's return, Francesca has to endure two hours of the configuration of the room changing, always leaving her with Richie but some extra party too. Her parents look at her in concern from time to time, try to involve her in their conversations. Francesca only wants to be left alone; you are alien to me, she wants to scream. They lunch together – a huge spread Anja has prepared in honour of the Maiers' final day – all German foods Francesca had proclaimed she'd loved, and it is excruciating. Francesca can't look at Richie as he fools around, trying to make everyone enjoy themselves, but most of all, trying to make her mother happy with the decision she's made to pull out of the danger zone. Everyone knows she's afraid of something, Francesca thinks. Everyone knows there's a cover-up going on. But it doesn't matter anymore, she'll have a new life soon, which will be no part of theirs; in a few hours she'll be able to forget all about her mother's lies.

AFTER THE MEAL, Anja announces she needs to go out to find something for her class at the kindergarten. She wants to escape, thinks Francesca – the fool! And then, to Francesca's great joy, her mother says she needs to pick up some presents to take home, and doesn't want to rely on the junk sold at the airport. Her mother makes two things clear without saying either: firstly, she'll be walking in the opposite direction to Anja; and secondly, she expects Alex to accompany her. On hearing this, Francesca perks up so much that her mother thinks she wants to come along too, to pick up some things for her friends at school, perhaps? Francesca smiles an apology at her dear, sweet Richie for almost messing things up, and frowns her dissent at her mother. She'd rather rest for the journey at home, watching TV with Richie. She gives her mother an order for a present she'd like for Charlotte, so as not to blow their cover. It's a doll she'd seen in a shop they'd passed on their way to underground, a really cool one with huge blue eyelashes. Charlotte collects china dolls, which everyone else thinks is weird at nearly fifteen, but Francesca gets it. The present has a message in it, to let Charlotte know she's sorry for abandoning her. One day she'll explain why she hadn't been able to let her best friend in on what's happening to her.

ALEX SCRATCHES his head at his daughter's behaviour: who'd want to stay in this sweltering little flat on their last day in Berlin, the last day of their elongated summer holiday? Only a teenager, he thinks with an involuntary sigh, forgiving her as he softly shuts the door behind him. At least Richie's there to look after her, to make sure she won't go sneaking off to find her friends without telling them. She'd be cutting it fine to make it across the city and back in time for their flight that evening.

WHEN, at last, they are alone, there is no need for words. They sit together on the couch, reflecting on the past ten days, and contemplating what is to come. A film is playing in the background, but Francesca isn't concentrating on the words, she's letting them wash over her like the sea, and she's sure Richie is too. After all, she doesn't need her German anymore; that part of her is about to fade away for good. By tomorrow it'll be dead, and the remnants of her short life in Germany will sink to her toes, where she'll shake them out of her flip-flops like sand.

She'll leave them at the shore of the lake at Wannsee, Francesca thinks. That's where they belong. And then Richie will take her hand, and they'll shoot up into the sky like stars and fly away to Spain together. She'll be a chameleon, and he'll love her for it.

SHE DOESN'T DARE LOOK at him. She feels so giddy with the air between them; she thinks she might pass out if she looks at him. They haven't been truly alone since that day at the lake, and now the sofa has turned into the canoe; once again they are marooned quite happily together. What would the girls at school think, wonders Francesca, her toes tingling. Richie's a grown man with a job, and he *loves* her. He must do, to go through with what they're planning. He must love her even more than Jay loved Lena, though she can't think about that – everyone must know Lena doesn't deserve to be loved, but she can't think about the reasons for *that* right now.

She knows she has to calm down. Richie would want her to calm down. She remembers kissing Antonio, in the old bunker and then later at the edge of the park, where he'd pulled her under a canopy of branches with him. After they'd finished kissing the second time she'd tried not to look down, as the ground had been littered with crisp packets and drinks cans and, disorientatingly, even a pair of shoes. She hadn't blamed Antonio though – *that* kiss hadn't been an ordeal at all.

Her left foot is close to Richie's right. He's talking about her new school year – asking about her friends, the subject she's doing best in – which is annoying as there's no one here to pretend to anymore. She wriggles her toes – whether to stop herself from getting pins and needles or exploding with anger, she can't tell. His feet are bare, and she has an urge to draw the strong curve of their bridge. He has beautiful toes. Suddenly, Francesca realises Richie's looking at her for an answer to a question she hadn't realised he'd asked. She smiles softly, her freshly glossed lips shining. She wills him to understand that none of that stuff matters now – it's just the two of them, alone in a canoe; they are finally and wonderfully themselves.

'Are you okay, Fran? You look a little flushed. Are you certain you didn't want to go for the walk with your parents – to get some air?'

Francesca shakes her head deliberately. You should have fixed the windows, she wants to say. Then it wouldn't be so warm in here all the time. And then it strikes her that perhaps he's nervous too; that perhaps he needs her to take charge.

She leans forward, and Richie sighs. 'We'll miss you around here, kid.'

To her surprise, Richie's grin clouds over. He talks quietly now. 'I thought there would be more time. I wanted to explain—'

We have all the time in the world, she wants to say. Instead, she asks about the window.

'Why won't it open?' she asks, gesturing to the one closest to her, so inviting with the street's ancient trees beckoning and the whole of Berlin laid out beyond.

Richie smiles and she thinks he'll say something about his terrible DIY skills, but in an instant he's shaking, trying to hold back tiny sobs that come out as hiccups.

'It isn't safe,' he says, his breath ragged so that Francesca thinks he might be having a panic attack. '*She* wasn't safe.'

'Alexandra?' whispers Francesca, engulfed by understanding. She whispers consolation like sweet nothings. *He can tell her anything.*

And, in time, he will.

He is curled next to her on the sofa, more like a small boy than ever. She will have her story.

'Anja will say she should have been watching, but it isn't true. *I* should have been watching. Things were difficult. Fragile. Alexandra was often angry. Angrier than any three-year-old should be. We didn't know what to do. Anja was often tearful. I should have done something for them both. I should have been home.'

She holds him until the sobs subside, and then, though she knows all the gods and all the ghosts of this city forbid it, she leans forward and pushes her lips against his.

27

Later, rushing to Antonio's bar, she doesn't cry as she'd thought she would. She may be burning up with humiliation, but she doesn't cry. The truth slams into her repeatedly. Richie hadn't kissed her back. He had moved away from her in horror, retracting himself as though he'd been stung by a jellyfish he hadn't spotted in the water. The horror of it! He'd looked at her with such revulsion in his eyes. Francesca stops running then – there's a pain in her side like a stitch, only a zillion times worse, and she can't move any further.

All she can think to do is to call Antonio. She finds his number with shaking fingers, the screen on the mobile suddenly too small, and when the phone rings on to voicemail all she can do is say his name and breathe down the phone like a stalker. She hangs up and rings again. The first day they'd met, Antonio had said if she ever got lost in the city again he'd come and find her. Only she's more lost than she's ever been, and it's obvious he's not coming for her. She remembers Richie calling for her to wait, calling from the hallway when she'd already been halfway down the street, his voice half-strangled with horror. Of course, she couldn't wait – she had to get out of there, and the only place she could think to get to, the only place she'd feel safe – was Antonio's bar.

Francesca's stomach churns at the people she watches walking past. They've committed nothing as monumentally and grotesquely stupid as she has this morning; they hold no shame as terrible as hers. They're clearly all busy, too – she's sitting in the street in obvious distress, and no one stops to help her. The only person who notices her is a small brown-haired boy who points his chubby fingers at her as his mother drags him past. He tugs at his mother's hand, trying to get her to look too at what he's seen, this girl who's scared and needs their help, but his mother pulls him on impatiently, and the child howls, staring back at Francesca with his hollow eyes.

She wonders what will happen when her parents return to the flat; what will Richie tell them? And Anja too – dear, sweet Anja, who had bought her the beautiful red dress, and had been so touched when Francesca bought her flowers. Dear, sweet Anja, who she'd stolen from and betrayed, who Francesca knows she will never understand. 'I'm sorry, Alexandra,' she whispers. 'Please forgive me.' But even Alexandra has turned her back on Francesca today.

The clouds that have been threatening rain finally open and Francesca manages to stand again, to stumble her way blindly to the *U-bahn* that will take her to Antonio, her last friend in this city. It's dark and cold underground, and today Francesca can't cope with the change from outside to in. The monitor on the platform tells her there are three minutes till her train. Francesca doesn't know how she'll stand them; she can't bear to be still. She waits alone, as far from the other commuters as she can, her thoughts jamming into one another like cars skidding on an icy motorway: she remembers the feel of Richie's skin against hers; her surprise that he'd smelt of coconut; and then, without warning, she is punched by the shame of watching Emilio sink.

Across the platform from Francesca, a train arrives and she watches five people casually alight as though today is a day the same as any other. There's a family among them, a girl and a boy squabbling over a chocolate bar. Maybe things would have been different if she'd had a brother, Francesca thinks. She remembers her father's expression when he'd come back to persuade her to come out with him and her mother for the afternoon and she'd refused – resigned but still, undeniably, a little hurt. She thinks of all the little snubs she's committed against her father – the times he's wanted to talk to her and she's pretended not to notice; the times he's wanted her to show some interest in some building or other and she's made it clear she's only tolerating his questions and his presence. It had felt good to ignore him; a point of honour almost. Oh, why hadn't she just gone with them? Her father's return had been like a second chance, but she'd been too stupid to see it. They'd have been shopping for last-minute trinkets, little presents to take home to let the people they'd left behind for the summer know they hadn't forgotten about them – when of course, apart from the briefest of moments, they had. Maybe her father had thought he could save her from herself; but Francesca had stopped that happening.

Her train arrives, and Francesca steps in, numb. She holds Anja's butterfly grip in her hand, puncturing her skin and giving her something to think about other than the black hole of time before she tried to imprint her lips on Richie's. She thinks of every possible route that could have stopped her, but always comes to the same end point. She groans for the shame of it. She doesn't know what she'll do if Antonio isn't at the end of this journey. The train waits at the platform, bringing Francesca's frantic thoughts screeching to a stop. *Can't you just leave already*, she pleads with the lump of metal and plastic. It's dangerous here; surely he knows this is where she'd run. She has no choice but to descend into this barren cavern and await transportation somewhere else. *Please go* she begs, and the only other passenger in the carriage, a lady with impeccable make-up and shiny red shoes sitting opposite looks at her uncomfortably, uncrossing and re-crossing her arms, looking as though she's appraising Francesca's sanity with each moment.

The orange light is on, telling Francesca the doors are locked, but the train appears to be stuck. A swamp-like silence unfurls between Francesca and the lady with the red shoes. Neither have anything to distract them from the other in this carriage that's not going anywhere. Francesca knows there's usually an invisible armour people wear, which keeps them somehow separate even when co-habiting the smallest of spaces. But today, either herself or the lady opposite has forgotten to dress themselves properly for the sharing of so delicate and public a space. Today, Francesca and the stranger opposite are undeniably, *awfully*, present to one another.

Francesca feels the lady can see right through to her murky soul.

Feeling so conscious of the lady leaves Francesca no room to think of what she'll tell Antonio when she finds him. And anyway, Lena has snuck into the carriage to join them and is smirking at Francesca. She could have told Francesca Richie wouldn't go for someone like her, if only the younger girl had thought to ask for her advice. And you only have to look at Francesca to know no amount of maturing would make any difference. She's not built for beauty; she doesn't have the free pass to love women like Lena hold.

'You're just a child, Francesca,' her mother chimes in, slipping her arm through Lena's. 'I thought we warned you to keep out of trouble. You don't need to be worrying yourself with all this. Come and get an ice-cream.'

'What are we going to do with you now?' adds her father, despondently. 'Here, I got you a cone and raspberry sauce. Your favourite.'

Francesca sneezes over the imaginary ice-cream her father is holding out to her. A great gulping sneeze that can't be ignored. The lady with the red shoes jerks in alarm, and at last the train starts to move.

. . .

CHOKED out of the underground the other end, Francesca treads the familiar route to Antonio's bar. She doesn't know what she'll do if he isn't there, and she can't think what he'll say when she tells him she's leaving. She feels a charge of relief when she reaches the road, and can see the bar looming out of the street, somewhere anyone would pass without looking at twice, and thousands of people do, but in fact the only place in this huge and sprawling city where Francesca can find refuge today.

TWO HUNDRED AND forty seconds earlier, Francesca would have burst through the door to see someone else sitting in her place at the edge of the bar, perched on the tall bar stool Francesca has always chosen. But now, all Francesca finds is a bolted door and the torn notice of the closure of the bar sellotaped to the glass. Francesca gasps. A world without this place is unimaginable. Meaner, somehow.

Feeling more hopeless than ever, Francesca pounds on the door of *Die Lustige Riesen*. It's too easy for the things you care about to disappear in this city, thinks Francesca, her eyes stinging with tears of frustration. People, places and dreams can get swallowed up without warning and there's nothing she or anyone can do about it. She tries Antonio's number again. His voice asks her to call back later, unless she's his mother. 'Only joking, I love you mum!' the voice says hollowly. It's a poor recording, and the words come back as broken echoes. Antonio is laughing on the recording, but this simulacrum of her friend's voice, a weak imitation of the real thing, only infuriates Francesca. She cuts the call without leaving a message.

FRANCESCA PEERS through the murky glass of the door, wiping her side's dirt with her sleeve. She can see two glasses on the bar. To her surprise, one is a sharp-edged cocktail glass, the kind she didn't know *Die Lustige Riesen* held. Next to it is the oversized beer mug Antonio likes to drink from. He hasn't finished his drink – he must have left in a hurry. There are only two places Francesca thinks she can find him now. As she pictures the first of them – the home he shares with Ingrid and his devoted mother – Lena's mocking eyes tell Francesca what she must do if she wants to find Antonio today.

THE ROUTE to Jay's kebab shop takes Francesca down a road she remembers, although she's not sure why. At the end, she sees the sign, and the arrival in the wrong Mommssenstraße comes back to her. She remembers the crying child at the window; her parents' hissed argument; the hypnotic beat of the samba. What if, she thinks, what if she'd followed the carnival that day, allowed herself to get swallowed up by the city in one giant gulp? Would it have been easier if she'd surrendered to the city that day instead of this?

28

For Richie, time stopped with the press of Francesca's skin against his. He has not left the flat. He has not left his seat. His mind back-flips through black-and-white segments of the past weeks. Helping Francesca make remarkable progress with her German, surprising her with the trip in the canoe, making her laugh over the news-papers at breakfast. She'd seemed such a shy young girl when her and her mother had first arrived – awkward, even, unsure of herself and lost somehow, younger even than her fourteen years in the foreign city. And Imogen had been so uptight that he'd just wanted to make sure the teenager wasn't lonely, that she wasn't left out of things with all the adult ten-sions going on around her. He'd never thought. Oh god, he'd never thought. His stomach drops and then lurches as he scours the images. Had he done anything that could be misunderstood? Anything to signal he felt more than he did? He'd known he was on dangerous ground when Francesca had come to the shop with that girl – what was her name; Lena, she'd said. It's his job to sell perfume, to let the girls and women try as many scents as they desire. It's a cheap store; they're mostly girls that come, hanging round the counter in groups, often when Richie knows they should be at school, sometimes visiting two or three times a week. Every so often he watches one of them steal something from the store – a small item of make-up say, or a sweet. Richie never says anything about the kids that steal. He's not the security guard. The security guard is a lumbering, lazy man whose biggest dream is a longer cigarette break. No, it's Richie's job to sell; but he'd caught a strange look from Francesca when she'd seen him there that day. Something in the way she'd looked at him had shamed him for a moment; it *is* a shameful job for a grown man to be doing, especially when ranked alongside a loudly successful architect and a woman who works on the bloody television. He should have talked to Francesca; made her understand. But he'd been waylaid by more immediate concerns. He'd been petrified Francesca would tell Anja some story about what she'd *thought* she'd seen. Years ago, Anja would have laughed off any stories Fran might have told her, but something had told Richie that this time she would have believed Francesca without question. It had made him sad to realise this, and so his first concern had been to wait for his wife to blow up at him. And when she hadn't, he'd been so grateful to Fran that maybe – just maybe – she'd misinterpreted his simple gratitude for a different kind of closeness. His stomach lurches violently again, and Richie feels old. Old, and sad, and suddenly very tired.

WHEN RICHIE WAKES, it is to the scratch of a key in the door – the prolonged scrabbling of someone trying to get in to a home that is not their own. At first, still hazy from sleep, he thinks he is about to be burgled, and flounders for something to protect himself with. Then Richie remembers Francesca, and the horrible gaping feeling in his stomach returns, only to be chased out by a great wave of relief. He hadn't thought much about what Francesca had been doing before he'd fallen asleep, there'd been so much thinking about everything else to do, but now that she's home safely, Richie is flooded with relief.

Of course, there's a much worse explanation for the scrabbling at the door – and if Richie were to weigh it up at the moment the door opens and

Imogen and Alex enter, he'd say that facing the two of them a few short hours before their flight home without knowing the location of their daughter is worse than being burgled. Far worse.

Alex and Imogen are chatting loudly as they enter the flat. Imogen is flushed from the strong summer wind outside, and she seems happier than Richie remembers seeing her the whole holiday. Freer, somehow. She's going home, where she can resume control of her beloved news programme, and her family too. They're going home, and miraculously, nothing has been broken.

Alex and Imogen have spoken while they've been out, and Francesca will certainly not be allowed the free rein she's been given here once they're back in the UK. Alex has been tasked with making Francesca understand this on the flight home. Yes, the holiday is finally over, and Imogen is deliciously, almost deliriously, happy. After trying so hard to keep Alex from making them come here, she feels she's fought the lions, and won. Imogen feels a rush of elation. Her daughter and her husband are returning home, unharmed. It's a feeling she used to get every time the three of them were reunited, however short the separation.

'I found the most wonderful doll for Charlotte, Fran,' Imogen says, giving Richie a grin by way of greeting, and upending a small mountain of souvenirs in the middle of the living-area-cum-bed-room floor. She's waiting for her daughter to be impressed by the beautiful white porcelain before showing Francesca she's got her one too, as well as several other things she'd thought Francesca might like. Imogen can never resist treating her daughter. 'Well, where is she?' she asks Richie, her eyes sparkling with a good-natured impatience. 'Fran, I hope you've got all your packing done!' Imogen yells, wondering where her daughter can be hiding. 'She's not gone off to find that boy, has she? Richie, you knew we wanted her to stay here, didn't you?'

Richie shrugs. He doesn't mean to, but he does. And at this laid-back, insolent gesture, Imogen's good feeling evaporates. She should have known she couldn't trust Richie to look after Francesca. She should know she can't trust anyone. 'Honestly, Richie. What have you done now?'

If ever there was a time for a calm, adult conversation, this is one of them, but with Imogen looking at him in thinly masked disgust, Richie can't think how to begin.

'I don't know,' he splutters in embarrassment. 'She's gone.' How to explain; surely he can't mention Francesca's kiss. What would they think? What would anyone think?

29

Francesca arrives outside Jay's shop, alone. Her heart is thumping. It's the first time she's ever been here completely on her own, and the place looks strangely solemn, the peeling letters in the window almost foreboding. For a second, Francesca imagines the building years after some disaster has left it abandoned and decaying. Francesca shivers and decides to just get the information she needs, and leave. She won't give Lena the time or excuses to look down her perfectly formed nose at her.

Francesca half-knocks on the door, then chastises herself for her meekness. Who knocks on a take-away door? She forces the door open with a shove. To her surprise, the shop is deserted.

'Hallo?' she calls. 'Lena?'

Nothing.

Francesca slides the bolt across the door, fetches one of the plastic chairs from behind the counter and sits, nervously waiting. First Antonio's bar is closed, and now this. It's a puzzle, and Francesca doesn't need another mystery right now. Okay, she hadn't really wanted to see Lena, but after all the effort of getting here, all the while pushing thoughts of Richie out of her mind only for him to seep back in like the sea crashing over the most insubstantial of defences, all she can do is wait, trying as best she can to ignore the pain in her head, the thumping in her ribcage, and the gnawing in her stomach. The clock Jay had once hung on a slant and never corrected tells Francesca it's coming up for three o'clock now, and Francesca hasn't eaten anything since the half-buttered croissant she had taken from Richie's plate in a fantasy of domestic bliss at breakfast.

Francesca would like to think her recent romantic humiliation would prevent her from eating anything at this traumatic and harrowing time, like she's read in countless magazines, and like the girls at school wear as a badge of honour, love being the best diet of all as the annoyingly slim Jennifer Collins repeats tediously often. Francesca hasn't had a chance to test out this correlation between love and her appetite until now, and sadly, it doesn't seem to be working with her. For despite everything, Fran is ravenously hungry.

Of course, technically she's earned more than a crust from this place, never having been paid for all the hours she's helped out while Jay's been away and, again – technically – her and Lena are friends, so she should really be able to take what she wants. She's not comfortable doing it though, and would feel a thief if Jay or Lena walked in right now, and so it's with burning ears that Francesca pulls open the fridge door and looks inside. She shuts it as quickly as she had opened it, and retreats to her spot in the corner. The usually spotless and brimming fridge is empty. There's a chilli-red trail of congealed sauce that goes right from the top of the fridge to the bottom, and there's a small pool of milk that has met the sauce in the centre of the middle shelf. Francesca remembers the cupboard she is leaning against, and, holding her breath, looks inside. Empty. It's as though someone *has* swiped the entire edible contents of the place.

RICHIE IS RUNNING down Bernauerstraße in his best work shoes. It is the first time he has run outside for years, and he feels decidedly self-conscious. The motion is wringing out the churning lurching in his stomach, as necessary as the final cycle on the washing machine, and Richie is feeling better because he knows what to do now. He has worked out the adult way to address the situation with Francesca, only that involves reaching her before Alex and Imogen do, and as they have a head start on him suddenly everything has become extremely urgent.

Of course, it's *his* city more than Alex's now though, and Alex and Imogen won't know the dips and shortcuts Richie is planning. As Richie had seen the day the family had gotten lost on the way to his and Anja's, Alex has relinquished knowledge of the city of his birth. Richie takes heart from this, and pushes on, despite his ragged breath and growing blister. With each shaky stride, Richie is more determined to find Francesca first and make her see that however she's feeling it's going to be okay.

As he runs, chasing Francesca, Richie sees the city in a different way to how he's ever seen it before. For years, in tandem with Anja, he has eked out his own route through the city, making the sprawling mass as familiar as his own small flat. Berlin has become his home through meticulous repetition, the daily re-treading of familiar ground. For eight years, long after the promise of the abandoned philosophy degree had faded, and he'd ignored his family's pleas to return home to Spain long enough for them to have given up asking, he has taken the same *U-bahn* to the corner of the street on which he works, the time of his departure varying by no more than seven minutes, the total steps he takes to get there varying by no more than three. For periods of time there is someone Richie comes to recognise on the route, waiting at the station or alighting at the same stop as himself – people who accompany him on his journey and feel almost like old friends (though he never talks to them, or wonders what their story is). One by one though, they have disappeared, and only Richie continues to make the same journey at somewhere between 08.05 and 08.12 each working morning.

Today, though, following the route he imagines Francesca will have taken, the streets become suddenly monstrous, every one of the hundreds of windows he passes harbouring unimagined danger. He can't possibly count them, can't possibly count all the households, the families, all the bodies the walls are hiding from him. The city he has adopted and adapted to with such care morphs into its true alien self. There is no room for him here. The spindly menacing trees and signs in a foreign tongue all tell him that this is not home.

The ache in Richie's thigh is burning now and he wants more than anything to give up, to lie down and wait for Anja and Imogén to compete in the cruellest words they can punish him with, but the thought of the myriad of dangers that could await Francesca keeps him going. He must reach the girl before something terrible happens.

AFTER SATISFYING herself that there is not a morsel of food left on the premises, Francesca has the forbidden but delicious impulse to explore the rest of the building. She has seen the kitchen and the front of the shop, but never upstairs, which Lena has jealously guarded. She knows from Antonio that this is where Lena sleeps when she is staying with Jay, that there are private quarters above the shop.

Francesca climbs the rough wooden stairs two at a time, on tiptoe to prevent splinters, a trespasser's flush on her cheeks. She feels oddly triumphant, knowing she would never ordinarily have been admitted up here. At the top of the stairs she pauses to take in her ascent. She hesitates, prodding her ribcage as though to check the part of her heart that stores pain. It has not yet begun to heal.

Involuntarily, she sighs Richie's name and then gasps and puts her hands to her mouth as if to shove the word back in.

She stands at the threshold of a large unpainted room. The only furniture is a mattress in one corner, over by the window. Spilt across the floor are magazines and food wrappers, reminding Francesca of the mess of Lena's grandmother's house. There is nothing of any value in the entire room – and Francesca's not sure whether there ever has been anything, or if she's seeing a room that has been ransacked, where whoever had been doing the ransacking had left in a hurry.

Francesca realises that what she'd thought was the beating of her heart is actually another clock that has been left behind. She is oddly happy to realise she should be on her way home by now but has no intention of going. She'll fall through the cracks of the building and the city, and there's nothing and no-one to save her.

Francesca walks over to the window, and as she does Lena emerges from the corner, a great armful of belongings clutched to her chest. She lets it fall, clattering on the floor, letters and toiletries, a cat's ball bouncing merrily.

'Urgh, it's you,' she says, wrinkling her nose at Francesca. 'You scared me.'

Francesca stares guiltily.

A silence stretches between the two girls, as though they are two tigers weighing up one another's strength.

'Well come on, then. I could do with some help!'

'You're leaving?' Francesca asks.

'There's nothing else to do.'

'What about Jay?'

'He's too late.'

First Antonio's bar, and now this, thinks Francesca. Is everything ending today?

'I thought you were going home, anyway? You're meant to be leaving soon yourself, aren't you?'

Francesca stutters something about her change of plans. But she can see Lena isn't really interested. The older girl is harvesting her belongings again, stuffing everything she can into the top of a bulging rucksack.

'Just help me, will you? I don't have time for this,' Lena hisses, just as the screech of a car pulling up outside can be heard through the open window. 'Great!' she says, and Francesca can hear the unspoken insinuation that it is her fault, that Lena would be away by now if she hadn't caught Francesca snooping. 'What are you doing here anyway? But I suppose you're bored because Antonio's not around.' She says all this bunched up in a desperate whisper, so it feels like the one long sound you get when you let the air out of a balloon.

'Not around?' repeats Francesca, following Lena over to the window, where they both duck down out of sight and watch two unusually tall men manoeuvre themselves out of a beaten-up blue car. The passenger man is talking into his mobile, his face sour and mean. Lena puts her fingers to her lips and gestures for Fran to follow her. Below them, Francesca can hear one of the men thump his fist against the door.

Lena curses softly, hoists the rucksack onto her back, and grabs Francesca's hand.

FRANCESCA DOESN'T KNOW WHY, but she feels it is deadly important that her and Lena make it out of the shop before either of the two men finds them here.

30

A ntonio thinks it is strange that the person he is drinking what may be his last drink at *Die Lustige Riesen* with is Anja. He isn't sure what she's doing here, but then he's never been sure why Anja has started visiting the bar, somehow always missing the hours he spends with Francesca. It's not a secret, exactly, just something he's never shared with Francesca (he expects it's as far outside the bounds of possible occurrences to her as it once was to himself). He's almost entirely sure that no one else in the two families suspects her frequent visits either.

It's an inconvenience that she's here today; Antonio had wanted to close up without a fuss; he'd known the end was coming for months: it should have happened years ago. The only thing keeping the place going had been a small inheritance his uncle had been paid. Never a great businessman, his uncle had ended up paying to run his own bar. Today was the closing of the door, the hammering in of the final rusty nail, and Antonio had planned to knock it in alone before attending the English exam that would be his passport to great things, though his heart said always *what could be greater than this?*

Instead, Anja is parked across from him, drinking the last of Antonio's improvised cocktails and trying to bleed some sentiment out of him with her wide, attentive eyes.

LENA IS SQUEEZING Francesca's wrist so hard it hurts. Francesca's skin pinches white, and for a second it is as though she has a sister. Maybe a joke has spiralled out of control; maybe a treasured item of clothing has been ruined; maybe a usually hidden heart has taken a pounding. If, at that moment, Francesca were thinking of yelping at the pain – which she isn't – Lena glares her into keeping silent.

She watches through the spindles of the staircase as below them, the first of the two unusually tall men shoves open the door, the bolt Francesca had hurriedly pulled only halfway across flimsy against his bulk, and calls several times for Jay –

without awaiting an answer, as though he's already been advised of Jay's fate. Francesca flinches as the intruder follows the same motions she had taken not seven minutes before – only in reverse, so Francesca witnesses a bizarre mirroring of her own trespass, where every movement is heightened with the lick of violence.

'Where are you, Jay?' Bang! The cupboard door hangs at a broken angle.

'You know we had an appointment.' The fridge door whines apologetically open, and there is a Crack! as the man slams his fist onto one of the empty glass shelves.

'You know what happens when someone breaks an appointment with us?' He reaches for the stool Francesca had moved to sit on, its unaligned position, she worries, alerting the man to their presence. Of course it wouldn't she thinks, he's hardly trained in forensics, they're safe – and then her insides go cold, and she reaches to the floor on either side of her, trying to feel the snagged embroidery of the bag she had grabbed before fleeing Richie and Anja's flat. It's not there.

Below, the man gives an odd shriek of glee at his discovery, and tips Francesca's few belongings onto the floor. Last year's school bus pass is among them. The man stoops to pick it up. Francesca feels a renewed pressure on her wrist – the bite of Lena's nails – though whether in comfort or fear or anger, she cannot tell. The older girl has not let go her grip, or moved in any other way that Francesca can detect, in all the minutes since the shop has been entered.

The tall man is still alone, and much as his presence downstairs terrifies Francesca, the absence of his companion is a source of a terror even greater. Where is he? she wonders, sensing the second man is the more powerful; that the one she can keep in view is holding off the real fireworks until the second is there to direct or play witness to the event.

Or, she could be wrong, she thinks, as the metal stool is swung as carefully and lovingly as a baby before being launched in the direction of the shop's grubby windows.

ANTONIO DOESN'T WANT to be rude. He likes Anja, and feels a brittleness in her that tells him she makes herself suffer more than she should. He doesn't want her to have to realise he's been waiting for her to leave, but when she asks him to mix her a fourth cocktail, his almost saintly patience is waning. He's heard all about Richie's party, and Imogen's sudden decision to cut the holiday short, and knows there is more Anja wishes to unburden herself with, but today – just today – he doesn't want to get involved in anyone's problems but his own.

Once, when he was thirteen and in the midst of a particularly eventful summer, Lena, Ingrid and his mother (the holy trinity, he used to call them) had joined forces to plead with Antonio to curb his habit of solving everybody else's troubles. He recalls with surprising precision his sister's warning, neglected until this moment: *Keep getting involved in the whole neighbourhood's problems, and one day you'll be swallowed up by them.* Of course, he doesn't believe it's true – that all the collected strife he's ever been indirectly involved in will turn into some kind of monster, but he wishes Anja – his friend? his guest? – would realise he has his own problems to see to today. It is, after all, the closure of his family's business, a day that demands a certain respect. He's pretty sure none of his immediate family will ever own their own business again. They are all, he thinks, destined to serve. Perhaps not Ingrid, he corrects himself. He knows she wants her own life, away from the suffocating grip of family. He will be the one staying home to placate their mother. It is no sacrifice; the world outside his tiny corner of Berlin holds little interest to him. He never holidays: *what is elsewhere that we do not hold in our own pockets?* his mother used to say.

'It's her own fault,' says Anja, staring at the

bottom of her glass.

Antonio's reply is non-committal.

'I don't know what I'll do if I don't have you to talk to.' Anja gives three short sniffs and begins to sob.

IMOGEN'S stitch hurts so much she wants to cry, but with Alex lagging behind, she has to keep the pace up. If she stops running, Alex will take that as permission to stop chasing, and the chance of ever making their return flight will disappear into the vista. They will stop by the next block to phone Richie at the flat, to check if Francesca has returned, but until that point there is only the pavement to eat up in their strides.

IT IS Lena who gasps at the broken window.

Whether it is this or Francesca's abandoned belongings, or whether the intruder already knows someone is watching from above, it is finally Lena's weakening which worsens their predicament. A fact Francesca finds oddly satisfying.

IN THE BACK room of the bar, Anja unsticks herself from the warmth of Antonio's embrace. This boy, she thinks, is the answer to all my problems. She has a great urge to unburden herself to him: the fear, the guilt, the pain of all the years since Alexandra has been lost. All trawled up by Imogen's reappearance and the strange, ungainly daughter she has brought with her. Anja knows her friend suspects she has not guarded the secret as well she should: that she won't confront Anja on this for fear of the answer, yet Anja has done her duty well. Fourteen years, and she has not spoken out once.

And now the family are leaving – safely on their way home, without a care for what they leave in their wake – what difference would it make to anyone? Speak now, and she would be free of the weight of the secret, free of the ghosts of the past, free of the ghost of her child. Free, finally, to mourn.

Antonio pushes her gently away, and Anja senses her time with him is running out, that his thoughts will have moved from the need to comfort her, to the time lost in doing so. She has listened to him list the many chores he must finish before the bar is closed for good and he must rush to his exam; the cleaning, the fixing, the rubbing out: all she can think is that once it is closed she will no longer know where to find him.

Recklessly and without ambiguity, she pushes her body once more against his. He is a young man. He will not resist.

31

As Richie nears the final stretch to *Die Lustige Riesen*, he counts the failures in his life. His worthless job, selling crappy products for a dead-end company. His large, loud family in Spain he no longer sees. His abandoned degree. His dead daughter. *He should have stayed home – forget the money. He should have been there. Every day, he should have been there.* And now this new monstrosity – Francesca the only child he'd let into his life since losing Alexandra, and look how that's turned out. He succumbs to the image that has been nudging his consciousness since Francesca had fled, picturing the teenager falling from an open window in a final cruel mirroring of his own daughter's fate.

Perhaps thankfully – perhaps not – he does not see the image in high-definition; he has nothing but his nightmares to compare the image to. Berlin's emergency services had been swift in removing all trace of the accident, so Richie had arrived home on the evening of his daughter's death, a man robbed, with no trace of how that had come to be. The impact as stealthily erased as her life.

Until Alex and Imogen's return with Francesca, Richie had also had nothing to compare his imaginings of what he had lost to. It is as though he has restricted himself to two channels of life, when everyone else has hundreds, *and* pay-per-view. Only now does he see, through Francesca, the friends his daughter would have made; the friends he and Anja would have kept. He had only known his new task was to protect Anja, and now, for this day only – Francesca.

Reminding himself afresh of the danger his charge could be in, Richie staggers on, swamped by his failings. His chest wheezes painfully. At least there is Anja, he thinks. He has never once broken his promise to her. He has not let their daughter's death break them.

BUT ANTONIO DOES RESIST, and Anja feels the bitter slug of rejection. After fruitlessly cajoling him (she does not believe he would not desire her), the rejection hardens to sharp anger. What is stopping you, she wants to ask, but watching him move away once more she knows the only answer can be Francesca. She wants to scream at her stupidity – and his. He cannot be thinking of the girl – she is leaving Germany today and will most likely never think of her little holiday romance again. This country is not important to her. Antonio is not important to her. The girl hardly knows who she is. *No*, she corrects herself, *the girl does not know who she is*. Apart from the girl's mother, only Anja knows the truth of this. For once, she weighs the power of her knowledge.

'She will come back,' says Antonio, firmly but not unkindly, as though reading her mind. For him, there is no humiliation here. He has made many advances in his life; the results to him are impersonal: the pain momentary, no more than losing a casual game of pinball. He plays with a good heart, and does not anger when he loses. And yet he is accustomed to the emotions of drinkers, and knows that if he doesn't persuade Anja to leave, soon there will be more trouble to mop up.

'Imogen will not allow her to. It's too—' Anja pauses, sensing Antonio is only half listening. '—dangerous.'

Antonio *is* only half listening; he's unscrewing the darts board from the wall, intending to hang it on the kitchen wall at home. His mother will protest at first, but there is nowhere else to put it, and she will want him home with her more than she will object.

Perhaps if he'd been paying attention, Anja might have stopped. She might have bitten back the truth for a few more years, or even forever.

'Don't you want to know why?' she spits, a fury she can't ignore building inside.

Antonio is thinking of the day of peace he will have tomorrow – the bar closed, his exam done. His future waiting.

'That girl does not know who she is. Imogen's right, they should never have brought her here.' Not if she didn't want that ridiculous little glass bubble of a family shattered. 'Alex is not her father.'

There. The lie she has laboured to keep tethered to reality has been set adrift. She does not speak her part in the lie; that revealing the truth is not without risk for her, too.

With her words, spoken only in anger and desperation, comes none of the relief Anja has expected. There isn't room for the rest of the story – how being her friend's only confidant had cursed her over the years, bringing nothing but sadness and resentment while Imogen had cheated her way into everything she'd wanted. How her early advice that Imogen should not have the child – and certainly not keep it – had been ignored and herself treated with an ever-increasing coolness. How Anja had felt little of the joy expected at the discovery of her own pregnancy a few months later; and how Alexandra's death can only be attributed to the curse Imogen had placed on her. She had thought Antonio would fix everything, but now she realises he is one more problem to add to the rest.

'I have to go,' she says sharply, and Antonio fights his impulse to stop her. He would try to solve this if he could, despite his own problems, but for once his sister's words hold him back. *Keep solving everyone's problems, and one day you'll be swallowed up by them.*

He heads to the kitchen, takes the disinfectant from the cupboard and runs a deep bucket of scalding water for the floor.

'FANTASTIC. We're going to miss it.'

Alex checks his watch. He is about to argue, but realises that if they do not track Francesca down soon, they will very likely miss the taxi Imogen has booked, and then very likely the plane.

'It won't matter to you of course, but I've already agreed to a meeting tomorrow. Honestly, I don't know who I blame the most.'

Very likely me, thinks Alex, *for making you come here in the first place.*

. . .

OUTSIDE, Anja waits for the alcoholic haze to lift. She must get home, and sleep. She does not think of what she's done.

FRANCESCA SCREWS her eyes tightly shut. If I can't see him, she thinks, he won't be able to see me. She shivers as the stairs creak under a man's weight, and Lena's nails draw blood.

32

Despite being practically doubled over in pain at the chase through the city, Richie is almost euphoric as he reaches the mouth of the road leading to *Die Lustige Riesen*. He is sure Francesca will be here; he is sure he will be the first to reach her. Then he will pack her off home safely to the UK, and everything will return to normal. For today only, the girl's safety is all that matters.

He sees the form of a female ahead and believes he has found her; before the confusion sets in and he computes it is his wife who is standing, tear-stained, a few paces from the road. His world comes crashing: somehow she has reached Francesca and heard some twisted version of events, in which he

had willingly seduced the teenager. His wife is fragile. This will kill her, he thinks. Now she has heard
those words, even were the truth hunted down and
paraded in front of her, he will never be able to
erase them.

He moves towards her, preparing himself to be
stoned for an infidelity he had neither thought nor
desired to commit. Her face is contorted in horror.
For once he can see the years they have passed together, etched onto her cheeks, her olive skin. Not
for the first time, Richie feels robbed. 'Give them
back,' he wants to scream at the world. 'Give me
back the years we have lived!' But it is hopeless. He
must start somewhere.

'I didn't—' he begins.

Anja looks at him, wildly. 'I made a mistake,' she
whispers.

'You've seen Francesca?' he asks, anguished.

She says nothing. Stares at him dully. Sullen.
He's seen this before.

He knows his wife won't like him asking this, but
he has to. 'Is she okay? She seemed so upset when
she ran off. I worried something might happen to
her.'

Still nothing, and he remembers the last time
Anja was like this, when all he'd wanted to do was
shake her until they'd both woken from the night-

mare. He wonders now if either of them has ever really woken from that day.

'I have to check she's okay. Is Antonio in there?' He peers past her, into the bar. There's no sign of the girl.

Anja throws her head back and laughs. The noise is flat and ugly. Gesturing his wife to stay where she is, Richie runs inside.

THE FIRST THING Richie notices is that the bar is empty. The second is the reek of disinfectant. Richie follows the gleaming trail of floor out to the small yard behind the bar, barely big enough for the storage shed it holds. Inside the shed is Antonio, standing next to an industrial sized bucket and mop. If he is surprised at Richie's visit, he does not show it.

'Where is she?' blusters Richie, his tone accusing though he does not mean it to be. He needs Antonio on side.

'Now? I do not know,' answers Antonio, truthfully.

Richie tries to hold his patience, but it is not the time for games.

'But she has been here?'

Antonio agrees that she has, his tone admitting nothing for free.

'And you just let her leave?' asks Richie, struggling to keep the exasperation from colouring his words. He had been so close.

'Of course,' says Antonio, taking care to keep an even tone.

The younger man's responses are infuriating. But how completely he had charmed the family just days ago! They had trusted him with Francesca, trusted he would take care of her. Momentarily dizzy, vertiginous at the picture of Francesca hurtling through the air to her death from some unknown apartment in some unknown part of the city, Richie gropes for something to hold on to. He strokes the cold metal of a hammer tied to the wall. It is oddly comforting.

'Why would I want her to stay?' asks Antonio, carefully. It would not be the first time he has been accused of an affair he had played no part in. 'She was best going home to you. She seemed ... unbalanced. Upset.'

Richie steps forward, knocking the steel bucket so the water slops over his leg.

'She said some things I wouldn't want to repeat.'

Richie flushes purple. The boy is talking now, and he does not want to hear.

'It's none of my business, and she probably should not drink so much.'

Richie splutters. 'You let her drink!'

'Of course, this is a bar!' answers Antonio, bewildered. 'What did you expect?'

'I'd expect you to show some responsibility!'

Antonio is flabbergasted. *This family*, he thinks.

33

This is it, thinks Francesca. I might actually die today. She has never believed death possible until this moment.

The man standing in front of them as they kneel like children at the crest of the stairs is Very Angry. She can smell the fury in the perspiration rising from him like the shimmer of heat on an August morning.

'The money!' he is shouting at them. 'The money!' Francesca cannot look at him; he carries too much cruelty in his body, tensed like an arrow, tattooed muscles bulging for release.

'The money?' he asks, and this time he is almost wailing, mourning its passing.

The man kicks out restlessly, like one of the horses she'd watched baking in the heat to carry

tourists and day-trippers through the Brandenburg
Gate. Just in time, Francesca ducks to shield her face
from his anger.

Lena is not so lucky – she swallows the shock of
contact, but Francesca feels her flinch in pain. Next
to the violence, the strangest thing is that after it
neither Lena nor the man acts as if the explosion
had occurred. Lena expects no apology; naturally,
her assailant will not offer one. Within a beat, the
scene commences as before. This time though, the
man speaks painfully slowly – as though understanding Francesca needs time to translate his
meaning – explaining how very accommodating he
and his friend have been. Their books are square;
their record clean; their actions blameless. Few
would have been as patient as they, he spits.
Looking around the bare rooms, he talks himself
into a frenzy at what would have happened had they
left their visit another day.

He jerks a slim silver mobile from the pocket of
his faded black jeans and glowers Lena and
Francesca into silence as he conducts a blistering
conference of war into his phone. Francesca learns
that the two men do not know of Jay's fate. She
gleans that their man has been instructed to continue to search the building.

Satisfied, he taps the phone back deep into his
pocket.

'You will tell me where Jay is?' he asks neither and both of them, his eyes scouring the part of the room he has not yet explored.

'You will tell me?' he asks again, respectfully this time, as though enquiring directions of a stranger.

He ambles across the room, kicks open an old cupboard; theatrically holds his breath and waits, as though expecting a body to emerge. The cupboard is by the window, the furthest point from them. We could run now, Francesca thinks, trying to convey the same to Lena. The slightest shift of Lena's body tells Francesca she thinks this is a bad idea. Lena is right; it is not time for the siege to end. Their interrogator spins round, grinning like a mad cartoon character. He had been ready for them to run.

Something changes, and without turning, Francesca knows that the Boss is here.

He walks calmly up the stairs – lighter-footed than the other, there is no creaking – and gestures first Lena and then Francesca to stand. 'He's not here,' says Lena softly, fixing her cool eyes on his.

'Really?' returns the Boss, watching Lena closely. 'Of course, that doesn't have to be a problem.'

ANJA SQUINTS INTO THE SUNLIGHT. Her head pounds. It hurts to remember what she's done. And that Richie is with Antonio. She staggers into the shop,

and like Richie, follows the gleaming path cut
across the grimy floor of the bar to the small patch
of land where her husband and Antonio are arguing. They are two men clinging to a shrinking is-
land. She overhears Antonio saying that he won't
repeat what she has told him. The promise should
afford her some relief. But she has decided there
should be no more secrets.

THE BOSS WATCHES LENA, weighing something up.
    'Nothing?' he asks.
    'Nothing,' she confirms.
    'And your friend?' He jerks his head towards
Francesca, as though an idea is forming.
    The first man interrupts. '...We could take a
small payment now...'
    'Nothing,' says Lena, dismissively. 'She's a child.'
    'Then,' says the Boss decisively, 'We are at a
stalemate. Your friend Jay borrowed what he could
not repay. He is a hustler. A liar. What is he...?'
    'He is weak,' fills in the first man, tattooed lions
twitching.
    'Thank you, my friend. He is weak in business;
weak in love. In both cases, he took what he could
not afford. Think of us as—'
    '—Bailiffs,' supplies his conspirator.
    'Exactly. And what would bailiffs do in this situ-

ation?' He leans towards them, expecting an answer. It seems an age since Francesca has spoken, and when she does the words are in her native tongue. Lena steps in to translate, but the Boss shuts her down.

'Perhaps. Perhaps not. You think I am a lawyer?'

No-one speaks. It seems even the impatient lions are waiting for the Boss' verdict.

34

Listening to his wife tell Imogen's story, *his* story, Richie feels a great chasm open. He has batted away the confession of her attempted seduction of Antonio, can't think of it now. All he can think is that Francesca must not hear this today – or ever. He must act for all of them. He will obliterate Anja's guilt, her sins cowering in the shadows of his; in saving Francesca, he will save Alex too. Imogen, he knows, has won a free pass.

Antonio is pushing forward, gesturing that they move out of the shed. But Richie can't let him. If Antonio comes out of the shed, there will be more words. This may never end. Francesca might return to the bar, Imogen and Alex following her, and everything will be a huge mess. Richie has already lost his own family; he won't see Francesca's de-stroyed too. He turns to look at his wife – the last time from this side of the chasm – picks up the mop he has been unconsciously holding, and, handling it like the butt of a rifle forces it hard into Antonio's face, stabbing the end into the bridge of Antonio's nose, his eyes, the sudden soft flash of stomach as Antonio falls backwards. Antonio holds his hands out in a gesture of confusion.

Richie turns again to look at his wife – she has moved outside and is kneeling in the grass, violently ejecting the five cocktails from her body.

Richie groans – a wounded animal, twice bereft. He feels himself falling and reaches into his subconscious for an image he has long since buried. His daughter, his Alexandra – and with her all the hope of his once young life – lifeless on the roadside.

He hadn't seen this, of course. He hadn't been there. *He hadn't been there.* Could only be there to pick up the pieces of what was left of his disintegrating wife in the weeks and months – the years – that followed. Oh, the inertia of that time. The tiredness of it. They had talked once of moving, of leaving the scene of the crime and the memories that coloured every moment of their life together, *even this*, but somehow, in a cruel trick, neither of them could ever galvanise themselves. They had been alone in a heavy fug of grief and guilt. Few visitors – not even Alex, and he remembers how that had stung. How what had happened seemed a stain, so great an aberration that even parts of his life that should have been disconnected from the tragedy were never the same again.

There had been no one to help, he remembers that now – and his shock when he had realised it. No safety net, no one checking they didn't succumb to the black hole of grief.

And now this. That there could have been another path his life could have followed – that Alexandra and the pain of her need never have existed.

He remembers Imogen as she was then, of course. Young and skittish. Lost in a foreign country, pretending a sophistication she could not possess.

Really, they should ban these gap years for all the damage they did. No daughter of his – but Richie swats away the thought, remembers his careless self as a young man. His brief flirtation – and even briefer liaison – with the young English girl.

And from that, Francesca. Living and breathing – teenage now – a daughter – *no daughter of mine will lose herself in a foreign country* – a daughter that had been stolen from him.

Antonio is still beside him – mumbling something about an exam – he's going to be late – and Richie could hit the boy, if he weren't bloodied already.

'You have to find Francesca – you have to get her to the airport.'

He screws up all his authority and the words are like stones, painful in his throat. *'It can only be you.'*

If he looked into her eyes, his daughter found again – so soon given up – he wouldn't be able to do it.

Of course, Antonio will go. Of course he'll throw away the year's work. His escape. He'll repeat another year, his prospects ever diminishing whilst Francesca Maier is saved.

'YOU ARE LUCKY. I have just received some good news. Go!' says Lena, imitating the Boss' deep tones. Elated at their sudden freedom, Francesca hugs Lena fiercely, then untangles Anja's butterfly brooch from her knotted hair and pins it to the older girl's dress. 'What will you do now?' she asks.

Lena shrugs. 'Find Antonio. Visit Jay.'

ANTONIO DOESN'T KNOW where he's going when he sets off in an ungainly jog towards the *U-bahn*, but once he's there that compass he has for finding someone in need does not fail him.

And so, a short while later, he bounds up the

small hill camouflaging the old bunker and hammers on the hatch to announce his arrival.

Inside, Francesca is huddled in a child's pose. He sits beside her on the cold concrete.

'I knew you'd come,' she smiles. 'Eventually.'

'Nowhere else to be,' he says with a shrug, though his exam has already started; his empty desk to be expected, perhaps.

She looks into his bloodied face. 'What if it's me, Antonio? What if it's me making a mess of everything? What if just by living I make everything worse? All my parents have wanted to do my whole life is to protect me – but what if it's me the world needs protecting from? And I can't go back. I can't. I can't go back to who I was before I came here.'

She's breathless now, and when she stands there's a strange power in her pose. The stance of a warrior.

'I can't get on that plane. I won't.'

Antonio sits and thinks, and when she asks what he knows she will eventually, 'what shall I do, Antonio?' he holds his hands out, offering nothing.

'You have to decide who you want to be, Francesca. You must decide.'

35

There are no words at Anja and Richie's apartment that evening. Without the Maiers, the place is suddenly cavernous.

In the middle of the night, Anja wakes. She walks through from her bedroom to the living space, rubs her cheek against an empty patch of wall, goes to the hallway cupboard, and takes out Alexandra's picture. She places it back on the wall, sits in front of it, and waits.

36

Saying her own goodbyes to Berlin as the plane takes off over the city, Imogen feels the city crowding in on her one last time. Perhaps she had had no right to find love there. Certainly, it had been a precarious time. The world had felt volatile, and truly away from her family for the first time, she had felt her actions could have no real consequences. She had lived a little freer, no one to please but herself, been caught up in the myth of the city.

Her thoughts turn to the beginning of it all, or something like it. The first day of her second job in Berlin – the hastily found placement teaching English at Max and Moritz kindergarten. She'd been travelling on the *U-bahn* after saying goodbye to her new colleague Anja. The train had been empty, and her carriage littered with drinks cans and sweet wrappers, as though she'd just missed a party. There had been a single blue balloon bobbing in the corner. Imogen had watched a giddy presenter gossip through the entertainment segment on the carriage's television, feeling happy. She'd made plans to meet up with Anja and her friends the following Saturday. It would be the first weekend since her arrival in Germany she wouldn't spend sightseeing on her own.

She'd been half-watching the monitor, and half-watching the slowly deflating balloon, when the screen had shown her images of a smoke-filled underground station. It looked identical to the stop she was travelling towards.

Imogen's first impulse had been to take the emergency hammer she knew was carried in every carriage and smash her way out of the train. She'd fling herself against the concrete, and crawl back the way she had travelled until she reached the safety of the evening air. But to her horror, Imogen found she could not move. Her right leg had tucked itself under her seat and would not budge, no matter how much she pulled and pinched and slapped at it. The only way to leave her seat was to slide off it, and once she had done that she found she could not stand. Her breath came irregularly in great uncontrollable gulps, like she was waiting for a violent at-

tack of the hiccups to subside; her calf was a welter
of bruises. Imogen had crawled to the carriage door,
and pressed her face against its cool glass surface.
The train had shuddered to a standstill at its final
stop, the one she used every day, and Imogen had
peered anxiously out, hyperventilating. The station
had looked eerily quiet. And Imogen knew that the
train would be travelling back in the opposite direction in a few minutes. That the picture on the screen
didn't fit this station. It had all happened somewhere else, to someone else.

She'd pressed the green button and stepped
shakily onto the platform. The place had been deserted, except for a teenage boy working in the station kiosk, half-asleep with a comic open on his lap.
Imogen had stumbled over to the kiosk, pulling the
flagging blue balloon along with her.

'Did you see it?' she'd asked.

The boy had looked back uncomprehendingly,
groggy at being woken.

'The bomb. Did you see it?'

He'd looked at her like she was crazy.

'Oh, you mean on television, in Madrid. Yes, I
saw it.'

Her hands were shaking.

'Did something happen to you?' he'd asked,
chewing his words purposely slowly, as though she
were sick.

And perhaps she had been – perhaps they all were, though no one talked about it. Who could act sanely in such a world?

Richie, so charming, and yes, she'd known Anja had liked him, even then. His interest had flattered her – and anyway, what could it matter, in this foreign land, the world in turmoil – before she had met Alex a few days later (snoring beside her now) and everything about him had been more substantial somehow, had eclipsed the brief affair with his friend.

It wasn't fair – she knows that now – knows that the smallest choices, the chances taken – *do* matter. If only she had been honest. What seems entirely possible now – a daughter shared between the three of them, a life in two countries – had seemed utterly implausible – *impossible* back then. Times were different. *She* was different. And Richie, of course, not broken. Anja strong and young and invulnerable. Imogen had stolen happiness, stolen a future, when she had run away home, telling Alex yes, she could love him, she could build a family with him, but only in her country and only by her rules. Richie so trusting, of course – only happy for his best friend on the birth of his daughter, sending such an extravagant pink teddy bear that for a moment in the hospital she had wondered if he had known. She flushes with shame recalling that bear, one of

Francesca's favourites, and how she had waited for the attachment to loosen with a new haul of birthday gifts – or was it Christmas? – before smuggling it out of the house, telling herself it would earn good money for the local charity shop. It had all seemed so *necessary*. Necessary to protect Francesca, to save this little family she had uprooted from one city, one country, and planted in more favourable conditions in another. She had almost felt smug each year Francesca had grown, the secret kept, the family prospering. As though her actions – *her sacrifice* – were heroic.

She begins to cry – silently at first, then a whimper. Besides her, Francesca stirs. Tears are streaming down Imogen's face, and she wills her daughter not to wake. She knows now she has been looking at everything all wrong. Each day she had escaped with her family intact, the lie and its consequences had only grown stronger. Each day had only added to the pain of telling, the pain of discovery. She dries her face, drops the gentlest of kisses on her sleeping husband and then her daughter.

When we get home, sweetheart, I'll need to talk to you.

ABOUT THE AUTHOR

Claire Wingfield lives in Scotland with her husband and two sons. She spent two gap years in Berlin, after university ended and before real life began.

INTERVIEW WITH THE AUTHOR

What inspired you to write this book?

My first job after university in the UK was at a publishing house in Berlin. Whilst I wasn't enamoured with my first office job, the city and the people I met there had a profound impact on me. At 21, I drank in every new experience and it wasn't long before I dreamed in the new language. I was earnest in learning everything I could about this new country – a more diligent sightseer than I had ever been before or have ever been since. Along the way, I met some wonderful people – some of whom have inspired one or two of the characters in this book.

It's now almost 20 years later and this book captures that incredibly special time in my life. I distinctly remember the pull between staying past the end of my contract and putting down roots there or returning to the UK. I have always wondered what would have happened if I'd stayed in Germany, so I suppose that was my starting point for *Saving Francesca Maier* – although of course, many things have changed.

You can see photos and notes from the trip that inspired this book at www.clairewingfieldauthor.com.

What has *Saving Francesca Maier* taught you about writing?

Well, I began writing *Francesca* before my now-8-year-old son was born, so it's been a long process. Some ideas just don't let go! I also think there's possibly a right time to complete a book, so my perspective on events as a parent now myself may have been needed to complete the final draft – the final piece of the puzzle.

At every stage of writing, there have been people around me who have inspired and supported me – I mention them in the acknowledgements and some of them may not have even realised they did so, but just by showing an interest in the book and inspiring me with their own creativity, they were an enormous help.

What are you writing next?

Having thought I was writing a standalone novel, the characters have let me know they're not done with me yet! I'm writing a follow-up book, which sees Antonio's sister Ingrid come to Edinburgh as an au pair, becoming embroiled in the secrets of the family she works for and caught up in their outrageous demands of her. The family is connected to Francesca's mother Imogen, so we'll also see how the rest of Francesca's story unravels.

MEMORY PROMPT

Have you ever taken a transformative journey? *Saving Francesca Maier* was inspired by a trip to Berlin when the author had just finished university in the UK, so the memories are coloured by youth, but a journey with the power to change a person and their outlook can happen at any stage in a person's life. Take a moment to think of the place or journey that changed you. Senses can be sharpened by a new and exotic environment, so think of the sounds, scents and flavours you encountered – as well as the people you met. Perhaps you'll want to jot down some notes. You may even have the beginnings of your own story or novel! (If you do, Claire's book of writing inspiration *52 Dates for Writers* is full of writing prompts, hints and advice.)

ACKNOWLEDGEMENTS

This book has had a long gestation period, and many people provided support, encouragement and feedback along the way. My thanks to: Scottish Book Trust and Liz Small, Hannah Adcock, Karen Barclay, Stephanie Brodie, Beth Chaudhary, Alex Christiansen, Shona Clarke, Elaine Coleman, Sophy Dale, Polly Davies, Tracey Emerson, Amy Goymour, Julia Gray, Noelle Harrison, Fiona MacDonald, Anna Muir, Kristin Pedroja, Ros Powell, Sarah Ream, Emily Stott, Michelle Sudworth and all my first readers. Special mention to the unwavering creative and technical support of my husband Kieran.

Don't want to leave these characters just yet? Find out about new releases at www.clairewingfieldauthor.com, where you can join Claire's mailing list and connect on Claire's social media channels. Share your thoughts on the story at <u>contact@offthe-pressbooks.com</u> or spread the word by leaving a review in the usual places.

o t p

52 Dates for Writers
Claire Wingfield

This essential creative writing guide will take you away from your desk, to return with new ideas, fresh insight, better writing skills, and a renewed passion for your novel. It's suitable for both those who are seeking tried-and-tested strategies for revising a novel draft, and those who would like to improve their understanding of the writer's craft – to learn how to write a book that truly satisfies readers – and generate a store of ideas before starting to write a novel. Each of the 52 activities for writers to get out and do – from climbing a hill to visiting a favourite café, from sampling a new mode of transport to taking part in a hi-tech treasure hunt – is accompanied by an essay on an aspect of the writer's craft, and practical exercises to help with writing or revising your novel.

Including examples from well-known novels, and a chapter on editing your work, '52 Dates for Writers' covers both the craft and business of writing – from how to write better dialogue and revamp your storyline, to how to write your synopsis like a pro and understand your market.

£7.99
ISBN 978-0-9575279-1-1

Printed in Great Britain
by Amazon

38850981R00175